CONSEQUENCES

INTENDED

Brian J. Lynch

CONSEQUENCES INTENDED

BRIAN J. LYNCH

Cover design by Colette Sybert

Editing by CD McKenna

First paperback edition April 2026

Paperback ISBN: 979-8-9987828-2-4

eBook ISBN: 979-8-9987828-3-1

DEDICATION

For Dad, Mom, Karen, Gavin, and Melody. I love you all. This is for you. I don't think this story would exist if each of you wasn't in my life. The knowledge, the playfulness, the worry, and the courage to do everything I've done has come from you. And definitely, all of the dinosaur-shaped chicken nuggets.

Additionally, thank you to the writing community. There are too many individuals to name, but I have to shout out Micah Campbell and Chelsea McKenna. There's some pre-internet, no content creators exist world where we didn't share our expertise amongst each other, but this wasn't the one we landed on. And finally, to Colette Sybert for her incredible talent in designing the cover for this book.

TABLE OF CONTENTS

CHAPTER 1 - The New Place

"And where is this one going?" Johnny asked. He was lugging a heavy box up the fourth flight of a seemingly endless set of stairs. "The weight room?"

"Oh, hush," Eliza responded. "That's just the first box." She was growing tired of the incessant complaining her brother was feeding her as they ascended each floor. However, the help he was providing while she moved into her new apartment *was* appreciated.

"Is the elevator broken?" Johnny's question came with immediate regret. He bit his tongue.

Eliza froze. "No! I—you know I can't. Not after—"

"Li, sorry. I know. But maybe find a place on the ground floor the next time you move." He chuckled, hoping to lighten the mood and steer away from the sensitive topic.

Eliza reacted without thinking. In a blink, she steadied the bin she was holding and took a swing at Johnny's arm. Her own scribbled message on the side of the box in his possession that read *Fragile* was ignored.

Johnny sidestepped the incoming threat, but quickly dropped his right arm to keep the contents of the box from tumbling to the ground as it began to slide from his grip. "Watch it. This stuff is yours, right? Wait. Right? You didn't take any of my stuff from storage, did you?"

Eliza sighed. "No. I wouldn't want any of that junk anyway." She thought of the ratty old cardboard boxes labeled *Tools*, some with water damage, most covered in cobwebs, that Johnny had kept in his storage unit for sentimental reasons. Nothing in them could hold up to what she had in her own collection now. She knew that vintage tools were durable, and sometimes the originals couldn't be beat, but technology had changed enough over the last several decades to allow for better precision for what she used her own for.

Finally reaching the correct floor, Eliza looked at the surrounding identically-colored brown doors, each marked with varying levels of scuffs and scratches, to find the worn brass-plated number matching the digits of the new apartment that she leased. After setting down her load, she fumbled in her pocket to locate the keys she had received from the rental office.

"Hey, did *you* grab the keys from the guy down there?" she asked Johnny.

He glared at Eliza. "What?" he asked flatly.

"I can't—oh, here they—never mind. Is this yours?" Eliza removed a hair tie from her pocket and showed it to Johnny.

Johnny shifted his head back and forth, his ponytail grazing his shoulders at the motion, and responded, "I don't think so. My hair is still pulled back. But, Li, where are the keys?"

Eliza reached in her other pocket and pulled out a small key ring. Holding it in front of herself, she announced, "Ah ha!"

"Cool. Can you open the door now? I'm about to lose this." Johnny shifted the position of his hands to the bottom of the box, otherwise it would end up on the floor.

Choosing one of the two keys from the set in her hand, Eliza slid the piece of jagged metal into the keyhole and turned it. "Think they'll let me put a keypad on here?" she asked while pushing the door open and entering her new home.

"Would that stop you from doing it anyway?"

Eliza shook her head while her eyes took in the view of the empty room. Tan carpet extended from the small tiled foyer at the entrance of the apartment with each edge abutting freshly painted beige walls. The far end stopped at sliding glass doors that allowed access to a small balcony.

"Li, move please?" Johnny said, nudging Eliza with the box he was holding.

"Whoops. Sorry. Hey, put that over near the entrance to the kitchen." She pointed off to the left side where she could just make out the refrigerator from her viewpoint.

Johnny looked at Eliza and blinked several times. Although impatient to get rid of the weight in his arms, he still felt the need to pick on his younger sister.

Eliza rolled her eyes. With feigned sincerity, she added, "Please?"

"Sure, sis! Anything for you," he said with a wide grin.

Eliza stuck her finger in her open mouth and made a gagging noise.

"How many more boxes are in your car?" Johnny asked, returning to the front door. He stretched out his arms and wiggled his cramping fingers. "There can't be many in that tiny thing of yours, and my car wasn't stuffed."

"Only a few more. I didn't have much left that I cared about after rushing from, well, after the last place." Eliza hoped that Johnny wouldn't take her comment as an invitation to discuss her old apartment or why she left. He already knew the story, there wasn't much that she hid from him, but she was done talking about it and was ready to move on.

"I—right. Sorry, Li. I'll go down and get them if you want to stay up here for a moment."

She looked around again, then turned to follow Johnny. "No. It's fine. I'll come. I wouldn't want you to have to go up and down *all* of those steps by yourself with no one to complain to." To herself, she added, "I can already tell this will be better."

"Look, I know you just got the keys to this place, but as I said before, if you need to come crash with Linds and I, we can make room." Johnny made sure he was facing Eliza and looking at her eyes while offering up his support. If he didn't have her full attention, she'd likely think his offer was insincere. A repercussion of several decades of joking with his sibling and the need for very few, serious conversations.

"As much as I'd love to spend more time with you two and my niece, I need to get past this on my own." Eliza broke eye contact from the awkward interaction with her brother and looked off to the side.

"The offer will always stand." Johnny stepped out of the way and gestured for Eliza to go past him.

Before moving, she said, "Your little speech took too long. Let me step into the powder room first. 'Kay?"

Johnny sighed in response and shut the door.

After a quick walk-through of the new apartment, Eliza found herself in the bathroom looking in the mirror. She brushed aside the long locks of auburn hair that had fallen over her right eye and froze as she caught sight of herself.

The elevator let out an echoing ding as the movement slowed to a halt. Eliza was accustomed to the number of stops it usually made while she rode from nearly the top floor of the apartment complex down to the main lobby. She didn't bother looking up from her phone to see who was joining her, knowing that if it was someone she was friendly with, they wouldn't hesitate to interrupt her.

The doors opened and a single set of men's shoes appeared in her peripheral vision. The squeak of the rubber soles coming to a stop on the glossy floor was the only sound in the enclosed space.

Eliza knew she was being watched as soon as the doors began to close.

Ugh. Why's he staring at me? she wondered to herself. Say something or hit the damn button for the floor you want so we can get this thing moving.

Eliza kept her eyes on her phone, maintaining her focus while feeling the person's glare on her, hoping they would take the hint and leave her alone. Noticing the feet of the other passenger turning in her direction, her gaze remained down as she started cycling through the pictures she took moments earlier while on the rooftop of the building; the dimly-lit city skyline in the background with the main focus, a small toy car on the ledge of the building, in perfect frame. While trying to find her favorite image, everything suddenly went dark.

Ding.

Eliza looked up from the floor of the elevator to find several people standing over her. Her head was pounding above her right eyebrow, and she had trouble focusing. The view above was a bright blur of light stretching from one side of the ceiling to the other from the covered halogen bulbs.

"Are you okay, miss?" she heard someone ask. "You're bleeding above your eye. Don't try to move. We'll get help."

Eliza shook her head to clear her thoughts and focused on the reflection staring back at her. She had dark brown eyes that held on to many difficult memories, but no matter how hard she tried, the past refused to let go. A pronounced purple and blue mark stood out against her fair skin above her right eye and a small line cut through her eyebrow. She moved the strands of hair back to their original position, an attempt to cover the fading bruise. Once satisfied, she walked out to find Johnny patiently standing by the front door. He immediately opened it.

"After you," he said.

CHAPTER 2 - Johnny and Lindsay

"How's your sister doing, John?" Lindsay called out from the sofa after hearing her husband walk through the front door.

"Daddy! Where were you?" a little girl questioned.

Johnny stepped into the living room of their two-story house where his wife and daughter were.

"Hi, honey. I was with Aunt Eliza. I was helping her move into her new apartment." Johnny turned to address Lindsay. "She's okay. Or is at least putting up a good front. If nothing else, it's closer to her shop. Though you'd think she'd just live there with all the extra hours she spends making those videos she's always posting online." Johnny thought about the large variety of cars Eliza had worked on and the associated tutorial and demonstration videos of each.

"Leave her be. It's how she brings in new customers," Lindsay responded.

"And probably psychos."

"Hush. I'm glad to hear she's doing all right." Lindsay put down her work laptop. She joined her husband at his side and asked, "Did she feed you after you finished?"

After a short laugh, Johnny replied, "She did offer! But I figured I'd get back here to eat with my girls." Johnny reached down and scooped up his daughter, sitting her on his hip. "Nilah, once Aunt Eliza is unpacked, maybe you can go visit with her. Would you like that?"

Nilah grinned and nodded.

"Good. Now, what do you want for dinner?" he asked the young girl.

"Chicken nuggets," she answered matter-of-factly.

"Hmm. Frog shaped?"

"Nooo."

"Tree shaped?"

"No, Daaaddy. Stop."

"Then what?" Johnny asked with a comically large surprised look on his face.

"Dinosaurs. *Rawr!*" Nilah held up her hands, created claws with her fingertips, and pretended to slash at her dad.

"Help!" Johnny shouted with a laugh. He gently put down Nilah and pulled Lindsay in front of himself. "There's a dinosaur after me."

"Oh no. I don't think so," Lindsay said while sidestepping the incoming threat. "You're not using me as a shield. This is your battle. I'll go start cooking those nuggets."

Lindsay walked out of the room, leaving Johnny to fend for himself.

He dropped to the ground and landed on his back, flailing his arms and legs in the air. "Ahhhh. It's all over. Farewell. Tell my daughter I love her."

"Daaaddy, dinosaurs can't talk. And I already know you love me." Nilah planted herself on top of her father. He let out a quiet "Oomph" as she wrapped her arms around him.

"Nilah's bath is done and she's in bed," Johnny called out to his wife.

"For now," Lindsay remarked.

"Yes. For now. She had a dozen questions about why Eliza moved. She said she liked her last place because it had a pool. Once I assured her that the new apartment had one too, she went down easy." Johnny found a spot next to his wife on the couch and plopped down.

"What did you tell her about why Eliza moved?" Lindsay's concern wasn't hidden in her voice. "Not the real reason, right? I don't want to scare her."

"No. No. Definitely not. Only that it was time for Eliza to find something new." Thinking about the bruise over Eliza's eye that she was doing a poor job of hiding behind her hair, he added, "I told Ni that her aunt likes new surroundings once in a while."

"Well, that's a flat out lie. She never would have left that last place without a good reason," Lindsay pressed. "She's lived there the entire time Nilah's been alive.

How was she able to get out of there so quickly anyway? Did she have to break the lease?"

"She said she'd been there for so long that she'd been renting it month-to-month. And I don't think the apartment owner wanted any additional bad press associated with what happened, so they let her out early. Eliza said they'd prorate the month, not that she cared. She just wanted out and to begin to try to forget." Johnny placed his hand on his wife's leg. He gave it a light squeeze. "She definitely had a good reason."

"I know she did, John," Lindsay sighed. "I hope she can move on without it affecting her too much."

"I'm sure she'll be fine. She can hold her own. That guy was just lucky that she wasn't holding a wrench at the time or he would have been the one on the ground." He swung his free hand around, parrying with the invisible tool.

Lindsay leaned in against Johnny. After a brief moment, she sat up straight and wrinkled her nose. "Ugh. You need a shower."

Taking a sniff of his armpit, Johnny invitingly asked, "Want to join me?"

"No. Not particularly. Go clean up first and then we can talk," she replied with a wink. Lindsay leaned against him again and rubbed her hand across his stubbled face. "And shave too."

Johnny popped up quickly, causing her to fall against the sofa. He looked back at the sound of the thump and chuckled before heading off to the bathroom.

CHAPTER 3 - Unpacking

"Where's the damn box with the damn pan so I can make my damn breakfast?" Eliza yelled while pushing piles of cardboard aside. "This is why I hate moving. I wouldn't have had to do it if not for that stupid son of a—oh, here it is." She pulled out an eight-inch frying pan from a nearby box and headed to the kitchen.

After placing the cookware on the stovetop burner and beginning to preheat it, she walked to the windows in the kitchen and cracked them open. The deep sound of a car exhaust followed by a blowoff valve release made her grin. She wondered if it was a vehicle owned by one of her clients. Eliza took a look at her watch, briefly afraid that she was running late to open her shop; her routine of the last several years broken by the move. Relieved when it was earlier than she expected, she said to herself, "Okay, I still have an hour and my commute is cut by more than half from here."

Eliza turned to the left, the muscle memory from spending nearly a decade in her previous apartment taking over, to reach for the refrigerator handle. Slamming her hand into a wall-mounted cabinet instead, she let out a brief yelp of pain, and swiveled her head around to try to locate her target. Finding the tall, beige, rectangular appliance on her non-dominant side, she opened the door to the lower part and gasped, finding the inside clean and organized, not a victim of years of various leftover food and condiments that were forgotten. She grabbed the butter, eggs, shredded cheddar cheese, and a green bell pepper out of the refrigerator.

For the second time, she reached blindly, now looking for her knife block, and grabbed at air instead. Eliza slammed her fist on the counter in frustration and stomped back to the box she retrieved her frying pan from. A muffled thumping came from the floor below her, and what sounded like, "Hey, I'm trying to sleep down here." Eliza took the butcher block from the box, pulled out the meat cleaver, and mimicked stabbing the floor before lightly shuffling her feet back into the kitchen. Just wait until you hear my car exhaust every morning.

Finishing the prep for an omelet and tossing the ingredients into the pan, she returned to the box labeled Kitchen one more time and began unloading the rest of the items. She pulled out several screwdrivers and a 10 mm socket. Eliza put them in the kitchen drawer closest to the entrance of the room and detoured to flip the omelet. After removing a stack of dishes from the box and now finding it empty, she kicked it toward the door of the apartment and placed the load next to the stove. One move later put the omelet on the top plate and had Eliza searching the drawers for her utensils. She came up empty after only two attempts, causing her to pick up the omelet like a cookie and take a bite.

"I'm not even going to attempt to make coffee in this place yet. With my current luck, I may never find the water from the faucet, let alone the coffee beans, grinder, and coffee maker." Thinking of the local cafe, Grinded Beans, she decided that she would make a stop for her caffeine fix on the way to her shop. She put the dirty plate in the sink and licked her fingers clean before checking her watch. "Perfect. I'll get that coffee and even get the shop open early."

Once fully dressed, and with shoes on her feet, she surprised herself when she easily found her keys near the front entrance. The small side table she took out of Johnny's storage unit was already coming in handy. Eliza left the apartment, pulling the door behind her and locking it. She made a mental note to install the electronic keypad as soon as she had time, so she wouldn't have to fumble with the key to the deadbolt every morning. She walked past the elevator door, averting her gaze, and continued down the echoing steps to the parking lot. Approaching a red and white striped Supra, she reached for the door handle of her car and slid herself into the seat. With the clutch pushed in, she pressed the button to start the car. A quick wave of bliss went through her as the Supra roared to life. The exhaust rumbled when she shifted into reverse.

The morning talk radio wasn't enough to keep her attention. Eliza swiped through the pages of icons on the car's multimedia display, selecting the option to stream music from her phone. The initial notes of bass from the first song reverberated through the cabin of the two-seater sports car and triggered another euphoric response through her body.

The coffee shop came into view before the song ended, leaving Eliza disappointed. She debated circling the block to kill the extra time. Fighting the urge, she pulled into the lot of the locally owned business. With over a minute left of the song, she chose to shut off the car and return to the music later. The neon sign in the window of the building beckoned for her; a lit-up cup with steam coming from it. As she entered the cafe, the aroma of freshly brewed coffee wafted into her nostrils.

"Hey, Eli," came a voice from behind the counter. "Same as usual?"

Eliza ignored the unusual nickname that only the owner of Grinded Beans called her and responded, "I like my coffee black. Just like my metal." She slightly bobbed her head at the same time to the music only she could hear.

"I don't know what that means, but one black coffee, coming up. Anything else today?"

"Na, I'm good. I actually ate this morning, but couldn't find my coffee maker after moving this weekend."

"Well, that's good for my business, I guess. So, you moved? Why?" asked the man. "You were in town before, right? Did you stay there?" He began to grab a cup from beside the coffee pot, looked at Eliza's tired face, then grabbed a larger cup.

"Just the medium, Oli," Eliza said, playing with the owner's full name, Oliver, in the same way he did hers. "I moved a little more to the outskirts. Cut my commute in half."

"After moving, I'm sure you need the large. No upcharge."

Eliza nodded and took the now-full cup from Oliver. She pulled out a few bills and handed them over. "Keep the change."

"Thanks, Eli. Hey, I might need to get my car into your shop soon. It's making a noise when I turn the wheel all the way to the left." He motioned the direction of the turn with both hands as if he was holding a steering wheel.

Not pausing to think, Eliza responded, "Sounds like a bad bearing."

"Maybe. I also want a new set of speakers in the rear."

"Easy enough," she said.

"Just don't put my car in one of your videos," Oliver pleaded. "I don't need anyone knowing that I drive that piece of junk."

"No worries. Everyone signs a release before I post them online. I record almost everything I do so I can go back to it if one of my customers complains about the work after, to prove it was or wasn't my fault, but I don't put anything online without their permission, and I never use names." Eliza blew across the top of the steaming coffee. She tried to take a sip, but backed away as soon as it touched her lips. "And I love your car. You don't see many two-door Integras anymore. They're all sedans now. Just keep up on your maintenance. Speaking of, need me to change the oil and check over everything else for you when you bring it in?"

"We'll see." Oliver looked toward the door as another customer walked in. "I'll let you know."

"Sounds good. I'll see you, Oli." She lifted her coffee cup in a gesture of approval. She walked out past the new customer who was more focused on what they were scrolling through on their phone than where they were walking. Eliza rolled her eyes when she noticed the logo of the hat they were wearing with its brim obscuring the person's face. Any division rival of her favorite football team typically caused a similar reaction. Before the door closed all the way behind her, she faintly heard Oliver being asked, "Is that your Integra?"

Staring out at the parking lot, she looked over at Oliver's Integra. "Some body work and new paint would clean that right up. The paint scuff on the rear driver-side fender is a dead giveaway that it's Oli's though." After looking it up and down, and nodding in approval at the simple, yet effective, modifications, her focus turned to her Supra. The look of disapproval cut through the air when she found a car parked next to hers. "A hundred other spots around here and they park next to me."

She glared at the vehicle; a car similar to her brother's older CR-V, but not quite the same. After a quick glance at the car badge, confirming it was a different make and model, she looked over the exterior of the vehicle. If it wasn't for the noticeable body damage, she would have sworn it was Johnny messing with her, parking as close as it did to the passenger side of her car. Once the momentary threat of violence toward her sibling faded, she scowled, "I swear, if they door-dinged me." Eliza took a look toward the coffee shop, realizing the owner of the vehicle was likely in there chatting with Oliver about his Acura parked in the row ahead of her. She walked to her passenger side and did a quick once-over. Pleased to find her door still in pristine condition, she looked again toward the coffee shop, then opted to get in her car and leave.

The music began immediately when she started the Supra. The distraction allowed her to return to her center. "Okay, my car's fine, that guy's an idiot, and I need to get my shop open. I better never see his vehicle show up in my garage."

Arriving outside of E's Auto Body and Repair, Eliza parked her car in her designated spot wedged on the side of the building and approached the front of the shop. The light blue paint on the concrete block building seemed to glow in the morning sun. She went to each of the garage bay doors, stopping at one to wipe some grime off of the polished white frame with the side of her hand, and unlocked the padlocks of each. Heading to the main entrance afterward, she punched in the code on the electronic keypad and went inside. Eliza flipped on the light switch and looked around the lobby of her shop.

"Ah. Everything in its place," she said, running a hand lightly across the different automotive parts lining the shelves as she walked along the wall. She stopped at one box pushed further back than the others and pulled it forward to align it with the rest of the items. "Okay, now everything is in its place." She checked the time, more as a force of habit rather than needing to know the exact minute. Her assistant, Allie, would be arriving soon to let her know her schedule for the day. Eliza kept a rough agenda in her head, but she relied on Allie to keep her in check when she got lost in her work.

After opening the door to the garages, Eliza peered in at the three bays, eyeing the two with vehicles sitting on lifts, and the third empty slot. Eliza paid particular attention to the Aston Martin Vantage F1 sitting in the bay furthest from her. The trunk lid still needed PPF and the whole car needed a wipe down, but after, it would be ready to go back to its owner. She recalled how difficult the splitters on the front bumper were to work with and noted that the carbon fiber mirrors didn't need wrapping.

The jingling bell of the front door of the shop broke Eliza's train of thought. She peeked over her shoulder and called out, "Hey!" when she saw Allie walking to the front desk.

"Hey, girl," Allie responded back. "Good weekend? How was the move? Did your brother help?" She added a playful wink. "Did he have to take off his shirt?"

"Gross. And he's married. And he has a kid. Keep it in your pants."

"Whatever. Just let him know that I'll tune him up anytime he's ready."

"I won't." Eliza dragged out the last word. "The move was fine. I still can't find any of my stuff. The new commute is nice so far." She started to feel like she was repeating herself. "I'll miss the old place. Most of it."

"I don't know why you were living in town anyway. It's not like your shop moved. You've been here for how long now?"

"Almost ten years."

"And you did that drive for most of that time?" Allie questioned.

"I had my reasons."

"Uh huh."

"It had a good view?" Eliza shrugged.

"Did the good view have a name?" Allie leaned in, hopeful for some steamy details. She had been the receptionist at the shop for over eight years, and now considered Eliza her best friend, but not once had Eliza mentioned a name from the same building she lived in. Allie was aware of other dalliances, but this one would be new.

Eliza had work to do and this wasn't the time for gossip. She finished the conversation by asking, "What's my schedule look like this morning? I need to get the Aston Martin done, but he said he doesn't need it for another few days, and the Bronco wants the muffler swapped, but that won't take me long. It's lowered though, so I need to get the bend on the pipe right so it doesn't slam into the axle when I drop it from the lift."

Allie's hope for a response to her question fizzled as she stared at the boot screen of the shop computer. Eliza was in work-mode now and there was no going back. "One sec. You know how this thing is."

"It's still working though, right?"

"Yeah. Well enough. Okay. You have . . . an oil change at 9:15, a set of tires and rims at 10, and at 11, the 2x12 sub box. Must be the one sitting on the floor back here." Allie used her foot to tap the side of a hollow box covered in thin black felt with two large circular holes cut out.

Eliza nodded at the list. "All right, sounds good. Do we have the waiver for the Aston Martin yet? I might start editing that video when I sit down to eat."

"Yup. It's here in the inbox."

"Great. Thanks, Al. I'm going to get started on the Bronco while I wait for the oil change to show up. Can you check the stock on the cold air intake filters? And when you're done with that, let me know if you find any funny videos to watch?"

Allie chuckled. "Sure thing, Boss. Oh, hey, on that topic, are you sure you don't want me to take over posting your videos? I can filter out the nasty comments, too."

"Allie, no. I got it, all right?"

"I know, but after—"

"Allie!" Eliza was abrupt. "I'm fine. I've been handling it almost as long as the shop has been open." She waved her hand in dismissal of the suggestion. "I've been dealing with comments like that the whole time."

"But—"

Eliza stared at Allie in response.

"Fine. But if you want help with it anyway, just ask."

Eliza nodded and went into the garage. What had happened in the elevator, and the subsequent move, showed a sympathetic side from her friends and family that she had never seen before. The sometimes misogynistic comments left on her videos paled in comparison to her attack. She could handle some nasty words on a screen, but the extra attention on her was taking her away from what she wanted to do most: get back to work.

CHAPTER 4 - They Need a Vacation

"How was work, John?" Lindsay asked, half looking up from her work laptop, but noticing the dried dirt and sweat all over her husband after he came home.

"I need a vacation," he answered with a sigh.

"Me too," Lindsay agreed, typing furiously. "I've got this last-minute audit to wrap up and it's using all of my brain power."

"Then it's agreed. Where are we going?"

"Huh?"

"Vacation. Let's go. Where are we going?"

Stopping what she was doing, and giving her full attention to Johnny, Lindsay asked with a puzzled expression on her face, "How? We can't just up and go. Would Nilah come with us? For how long? I've got work. You've got work." She stumbled over her words, finally finishing with, "When?"

"I've been thinking about it. There's that cabin we like out west. I already checked and it's available this weekend. We could ask Eliza to watch Nilah since she's settled into the new place. We could actually get some alone time. I'll wrap up at my current job in the next day or two, and I know you have vacation time."

Lindsay couldn't find a response and only blinked.

"What do you think? Want to go?" he asked.

A few seconds passed with her staring at Johnny before she finally put a verbal thought together. "The cabin is available?"

"Yes."

"Just us?"

"Yup."

"Do you think Eliza would be okay with watching Nilah? Is that a good idea right now? Can she keep her focus on Nilah? I trust her, but I don't—" Lindsay looked down at her laptop screen. "I really do need a break."

"Nilah loves Eliza. Eliza will be fine. It'll just be for a few days. Just a long weekend. And yes, we both need a break. So, what do you think?" Johnny's hopeful eyes stared deep into his wife's.

"Yeah. Yes. Let's do it." Lindsay still had a confused look on her face, but the smile was beginning to come through as she realized what some time away could mean.

"Perfect. Now, I need to shower. It's a hot one out there today. I can go get Nilah from camp when I'm done."

Lindsay eyed her husband as he walked away. He pulled off his shirt while leaving. The day's humidity left his long hair frizzy, causing it to fall down slowly as he continued on. Lindsay looked down at her laptop, then back up at Johnny again. She closed the lid and rushed after him. "You know, I got kind of sweaty today, too. I could also use a shower."

"Don't you have work to do?" he called over his shoulder.

"I'll finish it when you're out getting Nilah."

"Works for me." He grinned.

"Nilah, honey, what do you think about maybe staying with Aunt Eliza this weekend?" Johnny asked, placing a grilled cheese sandwich on Nilah's dinner plate.

"Yay!" Nilah enthusiastically responded. "I'll bring my new doll, and her stroller, and my monkey stuffie, and my piggy stuffie, and my new game, and my—"

"Whoa. Whoa. It'll only be for two nights. You don't need to bring everything you own, sweetie."

"And my favorite shirt, and some crackers, and does Aunt 'liza like applesauce? We have lots of applesauce." Nilah was nearly bouncing as she continued to talk.

"I'm sure she does. But I'll bet she already has some," Johnny said.

"Maybe we should send some," Lindsay interjected.

Johnny looked over at his wife and smirked. "Ni, you can bring some applesauce with you."

"Yay!" Nilah exclaimed. She got up from her chair and ran toward the pantry.

"What are you doing, Ni?" Lindsay asked.

"Getting the applesauce."

"You're not going right now."

"But I want to." The young girl pouted at her mother.

"I'll tell you what. Why don't we invite Aunt Eliza over for dinner tomorrow, and we can ask her if she's free to have you spend the weekend with her?" Lindsay posed the question to Nilah.

"Okay!" Nilah returned to her chair and bit into her grilled cheese sandwich. "Can I have some chips?" she asked with a full mouth.

Johnny shot his wife a glance. "That was easy. Nilah, I'll get them for you. Linds, do you want me to send Eliza a message or do you want to?"

"You can," Lindsay answered. "You should check in on your sister anyway."

"She's fine."

"Is she?"

"Yes? Probably?" He wasn't worried about his sister—nothing from his recent conversations with her made him think that she wasn't coping well. She was as quick witted as ever, and could still punch him just as hard. He was simply hoping that Lindsay would do the heavy lifting for inviting Eliza over. Realizing he was going to lose handing over the responsibility, he finished with, "Okay."

"Tell her five o'clock," Lindsay added.

"Yes, dear."

Johnny grabbed his phone out of his pocket with one hand while reaching to get the chips for Nilah with the other. He turned to Lindsay and had a look of deep thought on his face.

"What is it?" Lindsay asked.

"Is this actually a good idea?" he replied.

"It was your idea, and now I want to go. So unless you have a better option, I would ask Eliza first. She might be busy anyway. Or not want to."

"Not want to what?" Nilah asked her mom.

"Nothing, Ni."

Johnny began typing on his phone after pouring the chips for his daughter. "Fine. It can't hurt to check. And I'm just asking her about dinner tomorrow anyway. We can see how she's doing then, and ask her if she's free while she's here."

Lindsay nodded and began washing the dishes. "Nilah, when you're done, change your clothes, brush your teeth, and we'll read a book, okay?"

"Hippos!" Nilah responded, requesting her favorite bedtime book.

"Hippos it is."

"Eliza said she's free tomorrow," Johnny interrupted. "But might not be able to get out of the shop until 5, so she'll be here a little after that."

"Yay, Aunt Eliza! Does she like dinosaur-shaped chicken nuggets? I think we should have dinosaur-shaped chicken nuggets. I'll make sure we have enough dinosaur-shaped chicken nuggets." Nilah got up from her seat again and began walking to the refrigerator.

"Ni, where are you going now?" Lindsay asked, her hands dripping wet after putting the last clean dish down.

"I need to see if we have enough dinosaur-shaped chicken nuggets."

"We have plenty. Please go finish your dinner," Lindsay pleaded with her daughter.

"Okay!" Nilah ran back to her chair.

"Johnny, can you get her to finish, and get her ready for bed? I need to finish the last document for work. You distracted me earlier."

"That wasn't my fault!" A grin slowly crept up his face. "Yes, I'll get her ready."

"Thanks. I'll need that trip after this week," Lindsay sighed.

"What trip?" Nilah asked. "I want to go on a trip."

Lindsay locked eyes with Johnny, mouthed, "Sorry," and walked out of the room.

"Finish up, Ni," Johnny requested. "The earlier you get to sleep, the earlier Aunt Eliza will be here."

"Like Santa!"

"Yes, like Santa."

Johnny stole a chip from Nilah's plate and looked down at his phone. Under his breath he said, "I do hope you're doing okay, Li."

CHAPTER 5 - Tutorial Video 1

"I've already clay-barred this trunk lid," Eliza started. "It's really easy, but if you need a reminder on how to do it, check out my video where I walk you through the steps. I believe that was on my Supra." She paused for a moment, catching a mistake in her dialog. "I believe that was on the Supra. Before I changed the color of the back, making it red, with a layer of PPF." Eliza grinned and looked toward the camera she was using to record the new video. She spoke directly to it, rather than to her future audience, to make a note for herself. "Edit out the part about it being *my* Supra." Laughing, she added another quick comment. "That's the second time I've referred to it being *my* Supra, I need to stop." She paused to leave dead space on the recording while remembering that she still needed to publish the video of the work on her own car, and then continued. "I changed the color of the back of the Supra to red, using a layer of PPF. Because this is a trunk lid I'm working with, I don't have as much surface area to worry about. Not like a hood or front bumper would have.

"After the clay bar, I spray the lid down with alcohol and wipe it to get the clay residue off and any other remaining grime and grease. After the surface is thoroughly clean, then it's time to apply the PPF. I already have the piece I need cut." Eliza reached over to a nearby table and picked up a paper-like sheet the size of her arm span. Peering over the top, she continued to address the camera. "Before I peel off the backing, I want to spray the trunk lid with a slip solution." She laid the sheet onto the table again, picked up a nearby spray bottle, and sprayed the back of the car until the surface was completely wet.

"My slip solution is just a little bit of soap in the bottle and then topped up with water. Now I can peel off the PPF layer—just give me one second to show that." Picking up the sheet one more time, she began to peel off a clear sticker-like layer. Left in her hands was a two-dimensional shape of the car's trunk. When that was complete, Eliza put the new see-through piece on the trunk of the vehicle. "As you can tell, I already removed the spoiler from this Aston Martin. There are some holes cut in the PPF to match where the spoiler attaches. With a good amount of slip spray down, I can slide the PPF around to get those holes to line up easily." She used both hands to move the piece of thin plastic around on the trunk lid of the car until she was happy with its placement.

"Now this is the fun part. I'm going to peel up one corner first and spray it with my tack solution. Then I'll lay the PPF back down so I'm not pulling it away as I work. I'll take my squeegee—" Eliza reached over to the same table that housed the various spray bottles and picked up a hand-sized blue squeegee. "With the squeegee, I begin to push out all of the liquid under the PPF, removing the bubbles as I go. See how soothing this can be?" Eliza nearly lost herself in thought while watching as the liquid solution was pushed out from under the edge of the PPF with each pass.

Remembering that she was still supposed to be talking to the camera, she faced it and said, "We continue doing this until all of the bubbles are out. The trunk lid juts up some before the taillights, but that's not much of an issue to work around. For the badges—you can see Aston Martin spelled out here." Eliza pointed to the individual letters spelling out the name of the car manufacturer on the rear bumper. "Some PPF patterns, like this one, have the letters already cut out. Some don't and you have to remove the badges first, then re-apply them when you're done.

"As always, if you need a video on how to remove vehicle badges, look for the one I did previously. The Mazda MX-5." Eliza squeegeed the last few sections of the trunk lid, pushing out the remaining liquid from under the new protective layer. "Now that we're almost done, I'm just going to wipe off this excess liquid with a microfiber cloth. Everything's looking good. All the holes of the spoiler are lined up, and all of the edges look great. And if not, and you find a mistake, now is the time to fix it, because once this glue sets, you're going to stretch the PPF if you pull up anywhere. It's unlikely you'll get it looking good again."

Eliza took a moment to wipe the top of the trunk lid, removing the wet spots and checking her work.

"All right, friends. With that, we're done applying PPF to this Aston Martin Vantage F1. The owner of this vehicle will have the peace of mind that the paint on this gorgeous car will be protected for years to come. Until next time, I'm Eliza at E's Auto Body and Repair, right at the corner of West Victoria and Chestnut." Eliza reached over to the camera after allowing a few second buffer for editing to pass, and pressed the button to stop the recording. She turned back to the car to admire her work.

"Just need to get the spoiler back on, give it another quick wipe down, and it'll be ready for pickup. Then I'll finally get this garage bay back."

Walking back into the shop's lobby, Eliza was surprised to see Allie still at the front desk. "Hey, why are you still here?" she asked. "It's dark, you should go home."

"Yeah, it's dark," responded Allie. "I didn't want you walking out by yourself."

"You can't be here every night that I'm working late. I'll be fine. My car is right outside the door, and I'm not going to be getting inside some stranger's vehicle. I'm not a child."

"Uh huh."

"You know I have to record when the shop is closed so I don't have customer interruptions. Or the hot rods revving their engines outside my bay doors bleeding into my audio feed."

"I can do whatever I want," Allie said with a playfully scrunched up face.

"I'm not paying you for the overtime," Eliza huffed.

"It doesn't matter. I'm doing the same thing here that I'd be doing at home."

"Watching funny videos online," the two women said simultaneously.

"Exactly," Allie continued. "Anyway, are you done for the night?"

"Uh. Almost. I'll finish up the last few things on the Aston Martin tomorrow when I get in, but I just need to run back into the garage and double-check that I got everything. Since you're still here anyway, can you shoot a message to the owner and let him know that he can pick up the car tomorrow evening if he wants?"

"You got it, Boss."

Eliza rolled her eyes before poking her head into the garage and checking that the lights were off. The various aromas—motor oil, transmission fluid, and the lingering rubbing alcohol scent from applying the PPF—pulled at her nostrils, and tugged the corners of her mouth up with it. She closed the door and addressed Allie, "Ready to go, my knight of the night?"

"Let me get the computer shut off and I'll be right there." Allie came out from behind the desk and held her arm out for Eliza to hold on to. "M'lady."

The women giggled at the silliness and headed for the door. Pulling it tight behind her, Eliza locked the door, checked the padlock on each garage bay, then walked Allie to her car. "I'll see you tomorrow?" she asked.

"You bet. Have a good night. Safe drive home."

"Always." Eliza watched Allie pull the door shut to her early 2000s Civic before walking to her own car. She looked up at her shop's sign, no longer flickering after she changed its busted bulb when she noticed the light misbehaving a few days prior. Eliza quietly wished it were a couple weeks past, when her only worry was if the sign was properly lit. She climbed into her car, shoving away thoughts of her previous apartment while pushing the *Start* button of the Supra to bring it to life. Eliza picked the background soundtrack she wanted for the short drive home and shifted into gear.

He could only make out faint details of the woman getting into the Supra from under the glow of the sign above the shop. The lighting was better now without the broken bulbs, but it was still too dark to know for certain. He was positive the person he was looking for was not the one that got into the Civic. It seemed unlikely that she had been the one putting the videos online. He couldn't imagine that someone so knowledgeable in the automotive industry would be driving that beat-up piece of crap. No, it had to be the one in the pristine Supra; the car he'd seen her working on in one of the videos. Looking at the front of the car from across the street, it appeared white in the dim light. The one he saw earlier, only from the back, was red. The crystal-clear headlights nearly blinded him.

He first found the woman who called herself Eliza in an apartment building nearly a week ago. The accidental meeting happened after he came from out of town to visit a friend. Eliza was standing alone in the elevator as he was entering it.

Her face was down, but he recognized her immediately. His skin flushed at the realization. *Oh shit, it's her. It's actually her.* He wanted to tell Eliza how he had been watching her videos, and how much he dreamed of being in them with her. *How can I get her attention? How can I—*

He made a move toward Eliza, trying to get her to look up. *I'm here. See me.* Unable to get her attention reawakened a pain he had repressed for a decade. His first love, first need, becoming a ghost on the internet. The chat messages had stopped and he was left lost. But now, this one wouldn't get away. He could see her. He could *smell* her. If he wanted, he could reach out and touch her. *Come on!* It overwhelmed him. He took what he believed to be a calming breath and came up with a plan. He'd playfully nudge her; pretend to stumble. It was an action he could blame on the moving elevator. He could picture the scene in his head. Maybe then she'd look up. Maybe she would smile at him and they could talk endlessly about cars after. He moved. She kept her focus away from him. *Dammit, Eliza.*

The next moment, he saw her lying motionless on the floor. That's when the elevator stopped at the ground floor and the doors opened.

He stepped out, sliding past the few people waiting outside the elevator. They were all staring down at their phones or talking to each other. None noticed him slip by. He faintly heard a voice talking behind him as he rounded a corner. "Are you okay, miss?"

He hoped she was okay. He didn't want to hurt anyone. He just wanted the attention.

A drive through the town shortly after the incident found him at the corner of West Victoria and Chestnut. A pair of streets etched into his mind with a shop with a sign name that Eliza nearly sang to him. He never thought he would be outside of her place of business, but was happy to see that she did, in fact, seem *okay.* He never intended to find this woman that he'd been watching on his tiny screen for the last several years. This woman that he felt a connection with anytime he would leave comments on her online videos. Now that he found her, and had been in her physical presence, he felt drawn in. Real-life Eliza had a magnetism to her. On video she was his want, but now she was his *need.*

The Supra began to drive away. He thought about following her, wondering where she lived, but he turned his head in embarrassment at himself. It was unlikely that she lived in the same building that his friend did—the large complex with the elevator where they first met. That would have been a strange coincidence. She was probably visiting a friend of her own.

He had decided the previous week that he would stay in the area for a while. His job didn't need him. Financially, he didn't need it. He would look for a cheap motel to sleep at and find a way to meet her. Again. In a better situation. One that didn't end with him slinking out the door while she lay unconscious. Maybe he could think of more funny comments to add to her videos while he was in the area. More elaborate comments to draw out longer responses from her. He returned his focus ahead, seeing only tail lights in the distance. He put his car in drive. The sound of the exhaust leaking from the bottom of the car resonated through the vehicle's cabin as he began to head to his temporary housing.

CHAPTER 6 - Eliza's First Job

12 Years Prior

"Dennis," Eliza began. "Are we sure this is what we want to do?" She asked the question to her boss at Midtown Automotive while she was standing under a car on a lift. She was cutting into the exhaust piping of a Camry.

"'ey, look," said the heavy-accented mechanic looking over Eliza's shoulder. "This is what they said they wanted. This is what they'll get."

Eliza wondered how the dual exhaust system being installed on the vehicle would look when the bottom side of the car wasn't designed for it. "But—"

"Eleeza, when you have your own shop, you can tell the customers when they're wrong. But *I* want their money. And they're happy to give it to me." With Eliza taking a break from cutting the old pipe, Dennis traced his finger along the length of factory-installed exhaust on the passenger side of the car. He then ran his finger along the driver side mirroring the same path. "It's gonna look like ass." He stopped himself, then snapped his fingers to catch Eliza's attention. "Not because of you, 'leeza. Your work is great. I will be sad when you move on."

"Dennis, why would I go anywhere? I like it here. I like the other guys. You've taught me everything I know."

"That is not true. You already knew everything. All I did was bring it back out."

Eliza thought about the two years she spent working on an economics degree before realizing it wasn't for her and then applying for an open position at Dennis's garage. She aced every question she was asked by her now-boss, despite having had no opportunity to get her hands under the hood of a vehicle while in college.

"And you let me use your tools," she added. Eliza's arms were getting tired from holding the angle grinder to the pipe above her head, but she wasn't ready for the conversation with a manager that she respected to be over.

"And then I made you buy your own. See, you're set to go off by yourself."

"Are you trying to make me leave?" Eliza almost looked hurt by the notion.

"No. No. But you are better off by yourself. You are good enough to have your name up on your own shop. Not behind the closed doors of someone else's." Dennis changed to a more playful tone. "Now, get back to work before I fire you."

"Your name isn't even on the sign outside. And you'd never fire me."

"I will if you never leave." Dennis crossed his arms in an attempt to look menacing, but the grin on his face never wavered.

Eliza returned to cutting the exhaust piping before her boss interrupted again.

"You want to hold it like this." Dennis placed his hands on the tool and tilted Eliza's wrist slightly. "It'll be a cleaner cut."

"See," Eliza said. "I still need you."

"See nothing. Get back to work." Dennis walked away with a swagger, heading to a nearby garage bay where another mechanic was bent over the engine compartment of a different vehicle.

Eliza finally started cutting the pipe again, wondering how she would ever get the nerve to leave Dennis's shop, much less open her own.

"Eliza!" the shop receptionist, and Dennis's wife, yelled into the garage.

Eliza caught just enough of her name to stop cutting and looked at the older woman approaching her. She would never finish the exhaust work at this rate. Maybe Dennis *would* have to fire her.

"Eliza, dear." There was a dispirited look on her face that matched her tone. "Your brother is on the phone. It's your dad."

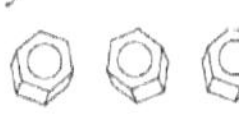

Present Time

Eliza answered the knock at her new apartment's door after looking out the peephole and seeing a delivery man standing outside with a clipboard.

"Sofa?" the man asked.

"That's me," she responded. "Want me to show you where it goes first?"

"If you don't mind." The man pulled out a pair of shoe covers from his back pocket and slid them onto his feet.

Eliza bobbed her head, impressed by the service already provided, and gestured for him to enter the apartment. She led him to an open area in the middle of the room and faced a TV that was airing a race between two modified street cars. "Somewhere right about here should work," she told him.

"Easy enough." The man took a glance at the TV. "Nice. I love this show. Did you see the last one? With the Challenger and the Camaro?"

"Yeah. That one was crazy. I didn't expect it to end that way, that's for sure. The exhaust work on that Camaro was amazing. I wish I could get my hands on it." Eliza's focus was now on the current race on the TV and less about where the sofa should go.

"Hey, you're not—" he started.

Eliza glanced at the delivery man, who was obviously trying to piece together the information he had. His eyes darted between the clipboard, the TV, and Eliza's face.

"I've seen your videos. Cool. All right, let me go get that sofa so you can get back to your show." The man walked out through the entrance. She saw him remove the shoe covers before the door shut behind him.

Eliza was used to people in the surrounding area recognizing her from her shop's videos. While happy with how well she did creating them and the extra business generated from the content, she was usually embarrassed when someone wanted to talk to her in person about them. At her shop, people could drop off their cars and she could remain faceless and in the garage. She preferred interactions like the one that just finished. An acknowledgement of her work, but no follow-up questions or comments. She could get right back on with her life.

The door quickly opened again. "Is there a freight elevator or just this one in the hall?" the delivery man asked.

Suddenly nervous at the mention of an elevator, Eliza replied, "I—I don't know." She hoped the man wouldn't ask her to help him find one.

"I'm sure it'll fit in the regular one. Me and my guy will be right back up." The door shut again.

Eliza stared at the closed door, tuning out the revving engines coming from the TV. She tried to push away thoughts of being in a confined space and helpless, but anxiety crawled up the back of her throat. What was once a daily occurrence, was now something she went out of her way to avoid.

CHAPTER 7 - Dinner with the Family

Knock knock knock.

"Aunt Eliza's here!" Nilah jumped up from the sofa, tossing her book aside, and ran for the door. She reached for the door handle before stopping. "Mommy, can I open the door?"

"Look out the curtain first, make sure it's her before unlocking the door, please," Lindsay called out from another room. Peeking around the corner to make sure her daughter followed her instructions, she grinned as she watched Nilah look out the window, jump up and down, and then unlock and open the door.

"Aunt 'liza!"

"Nilah!" Eliza scooped up her niece, holding the young girl close, and touched her nose to Nilah's forehead. "Too big. You're just too big. You've got to be . . . sixteen? Maybe seventeen by now. Here's my keys. I know your dad has to have already taught you how to drive." Eliza pulled the keys to her car out of her back pocket and held them out to Nilah. "Don't scratch it."

"Noooooo. I'm six. Not sixteen, silly."

"Silly? Silly? I'm not the silly one. You're the silly one." Eliza replaced her keys and put Nilah down on the ground. She began lightly poking at her niece's stomach, giving her small tickles.

Through giggles, the girl asked, "Aunt 'liza?"

"Yes, Nilah?" Eliza held her hands up, stopping the gentle roughhousing.

"Do you like dinosaur-shaped chicken nuggets?"

Eliza playfully gasped. "Chicken nuggets? In the shape of dinosaurs? Those are my favorite!"

"Mine too!" Nilah happily exclaimed. "Mommy! Aunt Eliza's favorite food is dinosaur-shaped chicken nuggets." She hopped up and ran off to find her mother.

"Hey, Li," came Johnny's voice from the side hallway. "Thanks for joining us for dinner. How was your day at the shop? How's the new apartment treating you?"

"Fine, brother. Everything's fine," she answered, blowing him off. "Nilah, where did you go? I want those nuggets."

A quick yell of "No, they're mine!" from the kitchen alerted Eliza to the little girl's location. Following the voice, she stepped onto the tiled floor of the recently renovated kitchen. "Hey, Lindsay," she said upon seeing her sister-in-law pulling plates out from a nearby cabinet. "Thanks for inviting me over."

Lindsay eyed Eliza, raising her eyebrow slightly. She shook her head before gesturing in the direction of her husband with her chin. Her short-cropped blonde hair fell into her eyes, and she blew it out of her face.

"What? You're telling me this was actually Johnny's idea?" Eliza asked. "Having *me* over? If so, what did he break? He should have told me so I could bring *my* tools over."

"I heard that!" Johnny yelled from the other room.

"Believe it or not, he's the reason that you're here," Lindsay reassured her. "Johnny! Your timer is about to go off."

"Yeah. I'll be right there. I'm just trying to get the stereo working. Again." A few music notes played before Johnny walked into the kitchen to join his three favorite ladies. He continued with, "Finally. I'm always fighting with—" He stopped and looked at Eliza. "Sorry. Clean versions of the songs." After tilting his head toward his daughter, he added, "You know."

"Yup. I know. So, you actually invited me all by yourself?" Eliza crossed her arms and raised her brow.

Johnny ignored the question and pushed a button on the oven to prevent the timer from beeping. "I hope you like lasagna."

"No. I wanted chicken nuggets," Eliza replied sarcastically.

"Dinosaur ones, Aunt Eliza!" Nilah added.

"Yes, of course," she addressed Nilah, then turned to Johnny. "So, what's up? What do you need?"

"I don't need—"

Cough.

Johnny looked in the direction of the obvious fake cough to see his wife staring at him.

"How about we eat while it's hot?" Johnny suggested. "Nilah, get the napkins for us, please."

"Yes, daddy."

After finding the oven mitts, Johnny opened the oven and pulled out a steaming pan of lasagna, followed by a large loaf of garlic bread. The aroma of each floated through the air, luring the family members closer to the dishes.

"Okay, that does smell delicious. Apology accepted," Eliza said. "Ni, where am I sitting? Can I sit with you?"

"Yes! Right here." Nilah pulled out two chairs at the kitchen table, pointing at one for Eliza to use.

"Eliza, what do you want to drink?" Lindsay asked as her head was in the refrigerator. "We got, uh, milk. And water. Wine or beer probably in the other fridge. Yeah, that's pretty much it." She chuckled.

"Water's good. Thanks."

Johnny began distributing plates of food onto the table. "Ni, please try the lasagna," he pleaded, putting a plate at Nilah's seat. "You liked it last time, but I have a couple nuggets for you too. Li, do you need anything else?"

"Na. I'm good. Thanks." Eliza eyed the dish in front of her. "Are you still using Mom's recipe?"

"Of course," Johnny replied.

"With the spinach added?" she asked.

"Only fresh. I know you don't like it from the can."

"Then you really must want something if you're making it the way that I like it." Eliza didn't bother looking up at Johnny and instead reached for her fork and began cutting the thick piece of lasagna with the side of the utensil. She stabbed at the smaller bite and held it up to blow the wafting steam away.

Johnny and Lindsay each took their seats at the table. Turning her focus to her husband, Lindsay motioned her head toward Eliza until he noticed and acknowledged her intent.

Speaking through the bite he put in his mouth, Johnny asked, "Li, so how *is* the new place? Find everything yet?"

"No. That's the last time I have you help me pack. Any idea what box you put my coffee maker in?" Eliza picked up a slice of the garlic bread and ripped off a piece with her teeth.

"Uh. Kitchen?"

"Wasn't there," she mumbled.

"Dining room?"

"I didn't have one of those."

Lindsay stared at Johnny until his eyes flicked to hers, prompting him to move the conversation along.

"Uh, sorry. If you can't find it, I'll come by soon and help look?"

"Sure," Eliza said. She picked up one of Nilah's dinosaur-shaped chicken nuggets and leaned it against the bite of lasagna on her niece's plate. Nilah began giggling at the dinosaur that appeared to be taking bites of her dinner.

"Anyway, everything's okay?" Johnny pressed.

"Yes, John. Yes. Everything is great." She stopped playing with Nilah's food and looked up at her brother who appeared to be asking her sincerely. "No, really. Everything's good. Thanks again for helping me move. Allie said she'd help next time, too. Make it go faster." Under her breath, Eliza added, "Or slower." Speaking to the group again, she continued, "It's not a bad place. It's pretty big too. Lots of cool stuff in walking distance and living outside of town is a bit cheaper."

"So, about that," Johnny butted in. "Could you, um, Linds and I would like to, uh. Could you watch Nilah this weekend?"

"Sure," she responded with no hesitation. "Why?"

"We'd like to get away. Take a break. It'll just be for a couple days."

"Of course." Eliza turned to Nilah and loudly whispered in an excited tone, "It'll just be us! We can do anything we want."

"Yay!" Nilah said. Half of a chicken nugget was in her hand and headed for her mouth. "Do you like applesauce?"

"Uh, yes, I do."

"Then I'll bring some!"

"That sounds good to me."

Johnny jumped in again. "And just in case you need to take Nilah anywhere, I think we'll leave you my car, okay? She won't be able to ride in yours, she's too small to sit up front, and the car seat is already installed in mine."

"I'd prefer hers." Eliza winked toward Lindsay.

Johnny took quick glances back and forth between the two women. "That one is going with us. We're going to be driving west."

"And you want to go topless," Eliza surmised.

"Top down, yes. The weather should be nice. Perfect for the convertible."

"Eh, you never know. You'll get into the habit of checking the weather a lot more with a car like that now." Eliza looked toward a nearby window, almost expecting to see rain at the mention of driving without a roof. "Let me know what day you're leaving?"

"You're sure it's fine?" Johnny asked again. "If you can't do it, it's okay. We don't want to pressure you. If it's going to be too much work or you can't—"

"Johnny, shut up," Eliza told her brother.

"Aunt 'liza, we don't tell people to shut up. Right, daddy?"

"Sorry, Nilah." Eliza looked at the young girl. "I won't say that. Guys, it's fine. I'm happy to watch Nilah. You two have fun, doing whatever you two do."

Lindsay cleared her throat. "Speaking of, I heard you have a date tomorrow?"

"I'm having a drink with your coworker, yes." Eliza's demeanor quickly changed from playful to annoyed. "Only because you suggested it. It'll be late. After I'm done at the shop. We're meeting at the small brewpub a block outside of town."

"That sounds fun." Lindsay leaned forward. "You'll have to tell me how it goes."

"Sure. I'll let you know." Eliza placed the last bite of her meal into her mouth and pointed at her full cheeks in an attempt to stop the conversation.

"He's nice," Lindsay added. "Likes to bike. Smart. Strong confidence. He's the guy we use to double-check some of our numbers."

Eliza politely nodded, and motioned for help from her brother. Noticing her request, he finished the conversation and asked, "Does anyone want a cookie?"

"Meeee." Nilah's hand shot up. "I do. What flavors do we have? I want chocolate chip. What do you want, Aunt 'liza?"

After a thankful glance to Johnny, and once she swallowed the food in her mouth, Eliza answered, "Chocolate chip sounds good to me, too."

"Bed time after this, Ni," Lindsay said. "It's late. Okay?"

"Okay, Mommy."

"Aunt 'liza. Can I have another hug before you tuck me in?"

"Sure, Nilah." Reaching down to wrap her arms around her niece, Eliza looked back to see Johnny standing in the doorway of the bedroom. "Good night, sweet girl. I'll see you this weekend, okay?"

Though a small yawn, Nilah answered, "Okay. Good night. I love you."

"You too, Ni. You too."

Eliza walked out of the room, brushing past her brother.

He turned to follow her, pulling the bedroom door shut behind him. "She really does love you, Li."

Eliza nodded slowly. "You made a good kid, John. You and Lindsay. I can't wait to have her turning wrenches in the shop with me."

"I'm sure she'd like that, even if it's just to spend more time with you. Anyway, you're really sure you're fine with watching her this weekend? We don't have to go. We can—"

Eliza took a swing at her brother's shoulder, connecting just below the clavicle.

"Ouch. Okay, fine, fine. Find another way to tell me you love me." He rubbed at the spot. "How do you want to get her and the car? Want us to come to your place?"

Eliza took a seat on the sofa in the living room after pushing aside a few small toys. "I can come by. I'll leave my car here if that's okay. It's probably safer at your house than having it sit in my apartment parking lot when I'm not home." She pulled her legs up onto the sofa, crossing them while continuing the conversation. "What time? My Friday schedules are usually pretty light. I might be able to close the shop a little early."

"No rush," Johnny said. He moved another pile of toys from an adjacent seat and sat. "I don't think we'll leave until later on Friday, but if you want to get Nilah settled in earlier in the day, that works. That way if you have any problems before we leave, we'll still be down the street. But if anything, I expect Nilah to be too excited just to be with you and she may never sleep."

"Me and her both. All right, I'll come by after I can escape on Friday."

"Sounds good, Li. Do you need a drink? I need a drink." Johnny stood back up.

"Na. I'm going to get going. I have some video editing to do before I get to bed."

"What car this time?" Johnny inquired.

"I actually have a couple videos I need to work on. I shoot a few when the weather's nice like this. Everyone's always getting the fun work done to their cars when it's warm, so I'll do a couple videos a week to keep in my backlog. Then I have those ready for when people are only bringing in their beaters for oil changes in the offseason."

"Like my CR-V?" he interrupted.

"Exactly." Eliza winked. "But I just finished recording one for an Aston Martin." She pulled her phone out of her pocket, flipped through a few pictures, and then turned the device around to show Johnny. "It's so far out of my price range it isn't funny, but it was a nice car to put my hands all over."

"Damn. Yeah." Johnny zoomed in on the picture. "Looks great. Did you get to drive it?"

"Only in and out of the garage. Unless the owners specifically tell me I can take their cars out for a spin, I don't do anything to risk the damage. But, yeah, I really want to finish the video for this one and get it posted. It jumped to the top of the list."

The concerned look that spread across Johnny's face caused Eliza momentary alarm.

"What, John? What's wrong?" she asked before understanding. "Oh. John, don't worry about it. I've got thick skin. I don't care what those people say on my videos."

"I know, it's just . . . I've read those comments. They're disgusting. If I got my hands on any of those people."

"They're just hiding behind a screen," she tried to reassure him. "It's nothing but words. None of them have the balls to come out and say that stuff to my face."

Johnny laughed at his sister's colorful language. "Sure. Fine. Just be careful, Li. I wouldn't want any of those creeps to actually find you in person." He reached in for a hug, startling Eliza.

She laughed. "Since when are you a hugger?"

Sensing the awkwardness, Johnny backed off. "Be careful," he reiterated. "Please?"

"Always. Let me go say bye to Lindsay, then I'll get out of here."

CHAPTER 8 - Tutorial Video 2

"Hey, guys. We're back today with a little paintless dent repair," Eliza addressed the camera that was set up inside the garage at her shop. The view behind her showed clear surfaces, except for the tools she was using, while all cabinet doors and toolbox drawers were fully closed.

"I'll be upfront about this," she said. "Paintless dent repair is not one of my specialties, and for bigger jobs, I usually refer out the work to a couple of different places in this area who focus on PDR. I used to even work at one before I opened my shop. I'll put the links to those below." Eliza pointed down, not at anything in the room with her, but knowing that once the video was posted online, she could add a list of links and recommendations for her viewers to see.

"This car here is owned by one of my regular customers. They were insistent that I be the only person to touch it. They brought in this daily driven, old-school, beautiful, Porsche 911. It's got a couple small door dings." After pausing for a split second, she spoke to the camera, a note to herself during her editing process. "Cut out this part where I move the camera to show the dents."

Eliza grabbed the camera from the table and walked to the door of the car. She held the camera under the side mirror of the 911, pointing it along the edge of the car and toward the trunk. She said, "You should be able to see some of the small ripples here. We'll take care of these two." Pointing at an indentation a few inches in front of the door handle with her freshly painted purple finger nail, she continued, "This one will be a little difficult, there's more of a crease in the metal. Something sharp hit this spot. But this one—" she moved her finger closer to the camera "—shouldn't be too bad. It doesn't look like the metal was really stretched much. I might get away with just popping it out."

Eliza reached for a water bottle sitting just outside of the view of the camera. She took a long gulp, coating her throat to help her continue. She stretched her back, the cracking from it more pronounced than she remembered it used to be. With the water bottle replaced out of the recording area, she cleared her throat and continued.

"Edit note to remove this section after moving the camera to the next dent," she said to her future-self while she moved the camera to the front driver-side fender.

"My customer is most concerned about the dent by the headlight here. The rounded part of the headlights on these 911s—" Eliza ran her hand over the top of the headlight, following the contour "—are one of the defining features of these cars. This dent really draws the eyes away from this unique aspect of the Porsche. The customer said he was playing baseball with his kid, just a plastic bat and ball, and after a solid hit, the ball bounced off right here." Eliza placed three fingers down flat against the indentation. "I haven't decided how I want to take care of this dent. Since I'm doing this in my shop, I might just take off the fender and work on it that way. The mobile dent repair places won't have that kind of space to work, so they'd leave the fender on and work at the dent from behind."

Eliza's habit of taking a drink between video segments had caused a few situations where she needed to use the bathroom at inopportune times. The water bottle sitting in reach was tempting her, but she decided to swallow her saliva and go on.

"Edit out moving the camera," she said to herself again. She carefully put the camera back on the table in front of her, placing it inside a taped-off square she used to make sure the camera kept her and the car in frame.

"As with almost every project we do involving the exterior of a vehicle, we thoroughly clean it first. We don't want any dust or small pieces of sand or dirt to get stuck under the tools when pulling the dents. I would be none too thrilled to do all of that work just to find I left behind a deep scratch. A clean surface will also help the glue that I use stick. I don't want it to release until I'm ready for it to."

Eliza shot a glance at the digital clock on the wall mounted next to another analog clock in the shape of a car tire. She could read both, but had a hard time finding the hour hand and minute hand camouflaged in the spokes of the tire clock. It was mostly there as decoration—a gift from a friend. Quick mental math of the time shown on the digital readout told her she had to go.

"Shit."

Fumbling to hit the button on the top of the camera to stop the recording, Eliza hurried to the door in the lobby of the shop. "I'm late. I got caught up. So much for thinking I could get my intro recorded tonight." She peeled off her coveralls, nearly stumbling as her shoes got caught inside the pant legs while stepping out of them. She tossed them on an empty table and continued on. "Thank God I'm ready to go and don't have to swing home first." After shutting off the light to the garage bay, she stepped into the shop bathroom and looked in the mirror. Patting at her hair, and laying several locks over her right eye, she then bared her teeth, checking that no food was stuck in between. She was relieved to find none, knowing she would need to re-record the intro she just finished if there was.

Eliza hurried out of the bathroom, shut off the lights to the lobby, and rushed out the door. Of all of the recent nights for Allie to listen to her and go home when the shop closed, this was the one that Eliza could have used her help with closing up. With the entrance door closed behind her, she locked it with the push of a button. A check of the outside padlocks to the garage bays assured her that the shop was secured. While making her way to her Supra, she pulled out her phone and typed a quick message.

Hi, I'm on my way.

She's leaving fast, he thought to himself. He watched the headlights of Eliza's car illuminate and wondered what he should do as she drove away.

It was earlier than most of the days he saw her leave the shop. Maybe she was going somewhere that he could intervene and talk to her. Try to get her to notice him, and acknowledge that he was as funny as he believed he was. He wasn't tired, and he had no other commitments. His car started—he didn't remember doing it—and then the car was in gear.

The Supra was still in sight. He would be able to follow it. The red glow of the taillights looked like a large beacon calling for him. He pulled out of the lot across the street from Eliza's automotive repair shop and turned onto the road. No other cars were between him and the leader, so could keep his distance. The Supra turned right. He turned right. The Supra turned left. After catching up to the same spot, he did as well. *Crap, was that a red light?* he wondered after going through the intersection. Looking in the rearview mirror and seeing no red and blue flashing lights, he returned his focus ahead.

"Where did she go?" he yelled out in a panic. The flash of brake lights ahead calmed him as the turn signal of the Supra lit to indicate that it was turning into the parking lot of a short brick building. A white metal sign at the entrance read "Belinda's Brewpub parking." He ignored the text below that mentioned a fine and towing threat, and entered the lot.

Before he could pull into a parking spot, he saw Eliza rushing from her car toward the entrance of the building. Stopping his vehicle in an open spot several aisles back, he stared at Eliza's car from a distance. "It's perfect. Just like her. No blemishes. No dents and dings. Curves in all the right places, and it sounds like heaven." His gaze was interrupted by the sound of a nearby car door. The smoke filling the air from the kitchen's exhaust created an alluring aroma that caused his stomach to growl. "I'm not ready to talk to her," he said, looking down. "I don't think I can do it yet. I don't know what I'd say. Hi, I'm—" Another closing car door stopped his thoughts. His stomach growled again. "Fine!" he said to his belly. Looking at the surrounding buildings on the same street and seeing the lights of each dimmed, he decided this was the closest place for him to get food. "Maybe I can keep my distance. Get a table far enough away from her, but not too far that I won't be able to see her."

He shut off his car and got out, walking toward the brewpub while making his path lead directly to the passenger side of Eliza's vehicle. He slowed his pace as he came up to the car. He didn't notice the red back and white front before; a perfect diagonal slant following the color change. Every time he had seen the Supra prior, it was parked face out at Eliza's shop and had the side of the vehicle hidden. The only times he had seen the rear end was in the dark and illuminated by the red taillights as it drove away. Moving his focus up to the windows, he tried to look inside. The dark tint created a mirror effect. The rough stubble on his cheeks and around his lips was pronounced from not having planned to stay in the area for as long as he had. He knew he didn't pack any shaving materials and made a mental note to stop in a store at another time. He wouldn't introduce himself to Eliza looking like he was. She would expect his features to be as smooth as her own.

A longer, drawn out growl from his stomach brought his attention away from his face. He looked up at the building Eliza entered. *Not now*, he thought to himself. *I won't risk her seeing me. I can find something somewhere else. Find a convenience store, get something to eat there and get a razor.* Rubbing at his sandpaper-textured cheek, he turned back to his car. A look of disgust washed over his face as he caught sight of his own vehicle. The door dings and hail-damaged hood were easily visible in the reflection of the overhead parking lot lights. Somehow, the bottom half was still nearly pristine. "That won't do either." He got in his car and chose a path to the exit of the parking lot that would allow him to pass Eliza's Supra. He drove slowly, following the body lines of the sports car with his eyes. Once out of the lot, he stomped on the accelerator. The tires spun as the grip broke loose when he turned the steering wheel to enter the main street.

"What was that?" the man across from Eliza asked.

"The spinning car tires?" she questioned with a raised eyebrow. The sound was hardly different from her daily dose of auditory automotive accents.

"I guess. No matter. As I was saying—"

Eliza leaned against the bar top they were standing at and began to tune out what was being said to her. The sound of the tires chirping outside caused her to think about the next steps she would need to do for her dent repair job. It wasn't often that she used those tools, but she was good at it and took pride in the work that she did.

"So, what do you think?"

The question broke her concentration. "Sorry. What? It's a little loud," she lied.

"I asked if we could reschedule. While I was waiting for you to get here, a last-minute request from this high-profile client came in. You gotta know the type. Has a couple million sitting that they don't know what to do with. Wants my expertise. Blah blah blah."

Eliza blushed and nodded while the man made unnecessary mouthing motions with his hands even though she didn't know anyone of the type. "Um, yeah, sure?" The guy across from her seemed fine, but her mind was constantly elsewhere. Usually on something with four wheels. If it wasn't for Lindsay's recommendation to meet with him, she would have never gone out of her way. It couldn't hurt to try again, and she did feel bad for being late, but who could blame her. The Porsche was stunning.

"Great. Thanks so much." The man downed his beverage, then slammed the glass on the table. He pulled a bill from his wallet, tossed it on the table, and began to walk away while still finishing his thought. "It'll get me a great big bonus if I finish it tonight. I'll call you," he said, thumb and pinky flush against his ear and mouth.

Staring at the silhouette walking out the door and questioning what happened, Eliza's focus changed as a waiter approached. "Can I get you a drink?"

Before facing the person asking the new question, she noticed the unnecessarily large bill left behind on the table by Lindsay's coworker. She decided to make use of the windfall and answered with a question herself. "Beer? Something strong, I think. Got one of those?"

"I can do that. I'll be right back."

Resigned to the lost night of being productive in the shop, she pulled up a barstool and got comfortable. She grabbed her phone while waiting for her drink to arrive and loaded her shop's online video profile. Swiping through the thumbnails of videos, she stopped at the one showing her own car. With a *Draft* badge next to it, she tapped the corresponding *Edit* button. *This one has been ready and I might as well get a new video out*, she thought. With her finger hovering over the *Publish* button, the clink of a glass on her table had her look up.

"It's an imperial stout," the waiter said. "Quite strong. Barrel aged, as they should be. I think you'll enjoy it."

Eliza took a sip, grinned, and nodded to the waiter. "Perfect. Thanks."

After a quick bow, the waiter walked away.

Eliza took another sip of the beverage before putting down the glass and returning her eyes to her phone. She tapped on the description box and began typing. *"Stay tuned for the first live stream video I'll do, next Monday evening. Remember to subscribe for updates."* She pressed the *Publish* button and placed her phone in her pocket. Picking up the pint glass, her thoughts drifted to the repairs on the Porsche 911 while taking a long swig of the thick dark liquid.

CHAPTER 9 - Nilah's Camp

"Ready for your day at camp, Ni?" Johnny asked his daughter after stopping his vehicle in the parking lot of Nilah's weekday summer destination.

"I think so," she answered timidly, unclipping herself from her car seat. "But I want to go to Aunt Eliza's."

"Only a couple more days," he reassured Nilah. "I'll tell you what, how about you stay home with us on Friday morning while Mommy and I work on packing, and we'll all be ready when Aunt Eliza gets there. How does that sound?"

Nilah grinned wide and bounced in her seat. "Yes! Aunt Eliza's. Aunt Eliza's. Aunt Eliza's. Yay!"

"Great. Hey, okay, calm down." He looked at Nilah, using his hands to try to emphasize his request for her to be still. "Now, let's get you inside so I can get to work."

The two climbed out of the CR-V, Nilah having to step down carefully from the taller height of the vehicle, and began walking toward the building that had bright rainbow-colored letters in every window.

During the walk, Johnny asked, "You have everything you need, right? You already have on your swimsuit under your clothes?"

"Yup. It's a pool day!" Nilah tried to purse her lips to look like a fish, but they wouldn't stay together.

"A towel in your backpack?" Johnny stepped behind his daughter while she continued forward and unzipped the bag to make sure she had what she needed.

"Yes, Daaaddy. Mommy put my goggles in there, too." She wiggled around to try to get her father to stop messing with her bag while she was walking.

"Okay, okay. Work on keeping your legs up while you're kicking when swimming." Johnny was appreciative that the camp that Nilah was in offered a weekly swim lesson, knowing that at some point he and Lindsay would take Nilah to the cabin on the lake that they enjoyed. If Nilah knew how to swim, it would put their mind at ease. "Someday you might be faster than Mommy when you're in the pool."

"Nuh uh."

"Yuh huh. Mommy used to swim all the time when she was still in school. She was one of the fastest. If you keep practicing, you might be one of the fastest too. Wouldn't you like that?"

Nilah nodded as they walked inside.

Johnny stopped his daughter before she made it to her group. "All right, sweetie. Have a good day and I'll see you later. Okay?"

Nilah smiled and began to head off toward her friends.

"Hey, no hug and kiss?"

The girl turned back around and wrapped her arms around her crouched father's neck. She planted a kiss on his cheek. "Bye!" she said and took off.

"Bye!" Johnny called out after her. "I love you."

"What are you drawing, Nilah?" the teacher standing next to her asked, while looking at the paper on the table.

"Me and my Aunt 'liza." Nilah grabbed the brown colored pencil and began to color in the hair of the taller person in the drawing.

"And what are you two doing?" the teacher asked, hoping for something more descriptive.

"We're having fun together!" After finishing with the brown colored pencil, Nilah picked up a red one and colored the hair of the smaller person on the drawing. "I'm going to spend the night with her. It's going to be fun!"

"That's great, Nilah. Good job. I hope you have a great time."

The teacher moved on to the next child, telling them, "We don't eat the glue. How did you get the glue anyway? We're just using crayons, colored pencils, and paper. Please put that down."

Nilah continued using the red colored pencil after finishing with the hair in the drawing to make a red heart that encompassed both of the stick-figured versions of her and her aunt.

CHAPTER 10 - The Police

"Ms. Banding," the official-sounding voice said. Eliza moved her phone away from her ear as the words coming from it were deafening this early in the morning. She was preparing the tools in the garage in her shop that she would need for her next job. "We received the security footage from the apartment complex from the day of your attack. Could you come down to the station and review it with us?"

She didn't have the words to reply. The sudden, unexpected rush of the memory of waking up on the cold tile floor of the elevator shut off the connection between her brain and her mouth.

"Ms. Banding? Are you there?"

"Eh?" The sound Eliza made allowed her to speak again.

"Ms. Banding?"

"Uh. Yes. I'm here. I'm sorry. Who is this?" Finally operating again on all cylinders, Eliza realized she answered the phone from the unknown number assuming it was a customer of hers.

"Ms. Banding, this is Officer Chapel. We have the security video from the day you were attacked. Could you please come to the station at your earliest convenience? We need your help to identify your attacker."

"Um. Yes. Officer . . . Officer?" Her mind was racing, but not entirely on the topic of the phone call. She hated these kinds of surprises, even more so now, and she wasn't catching everything being said to her.

"Chapel."

"Yes, Officer Chapel. I'll, uh— When I take my lunch break today, I can come." Eliza closed her eyes, trying to quickly review what she could remember of her plans at the shop for the day. "That should be okay. Is that okay?"

"Yes, Ms. Banding. Ask for me when you arrive. Thank you for your time."

The call ended with Eliza staring blankly at the screen of her phone.

"Who was that, E?" Allie asked as soon as the phone left Eliza's ear. She was standing at the entrance for the garage bays, waiting patiently to speak with Eliza. "What are you doing during your lunch break? Since when do you actually take a lunch break?"

"Officer Chapel." After the phone call, Eliza once again failed to put together complete sentences. "Elevator. Apartment."

"'kay? Officer Chapel, in the apartment." Allie squinched her face. "With a wrench?"

"What?"

"Nothing, E. Are you all right?" Allie began to worry.

Turning and focusing on her receptionist, Eliza was finally able to string together a coherent thought after she pushed down the anxiousness building inside of her. She dreaded the idea of seeing what happened to her from an outside point of view. "Yeah. Yes. I'm all right. Um, remember the thing in the elevator?"

"Of course, E. I came and got you from the hospital, right?"

"Right, yeah. Right. Anyway, that was the police, and they got the security footage from that day. They want me to come watch it with them. I guess they want to see if I recognize the person, that, you know."

"Oh, Eliza, I'm sorry. Do you want me to come with you?" Allie moved closer to Eliza, questioning if she needed to hold onto her friend.

Eliza was caught off guard by the use of her full first name. Allie had only ever called her by the name displayed on the outside of her shop or a variety of pet names—E, or on other occasions, just Boss. "What? Oh, no. No. I need you to stay here and keep the shop open. I have a small gap in my day." Eliza paused. "Right? Can you check that for me?"

The two women went to the lobby of the shop, so Allie could check the calendar on the computer.

"You're right. Nothing between 11:30 and 12:30," Allie reassured Eliza.

"Good. I'll go to the police station then, but I still need you here. I'm not letting this affect my life, and definitely not my business. I'm not closing just because some dumb son-of-a-bitch caught me blindsided." The anger in Eliza's voice started to take over her normally soothing tone. "He better hope I don't get a hold of him before the cops do. I'll grab the largest breaker bar I have and give him a matching welt over his eye." She unintentionally rubbed at the eyebrow above her right eye with her right hand while swinging her left hand around, as if she was holding a tennis racket. "I'll make sure he never gets back up."

Allie held her tongue while watching her boss show more raw emotion than she had ever seen. The last time Eliza was even a little mad was right after a customer left the shop while complaining about the work she had done, with him knowing full well that it wasn't her fault. Prior to that, a tire had unexpectedly dropped on Eliza's foot while it was standing upright. In the process of falling, the tire clipped Eliza's secondary video recording camera, causing it to also fall. The camera was smashed, rendering it unusable during the filming of a brake pad replacement tutorial. After a quick cursing session, and Allie checking in on the noise, Eliza went right back to work.

"Asshole," Eliza finished. Her demeanor quickly changed, now focused on her work. "What's first for today?" she asked her receptionist and best friend, happy to have someone that would listen to her vent.

Allie smirked. "Something you might need that breaker bar for. An axle replacement on a manual transmission Nissan."

Eliza was always happy when Allie understood what tools were involved in the various work that came into the shop. She responded simply with, "Got it. Thanks."

"Sure thing, Boss."

Eliza shook her head, a mischievous response at being called *Boss*. She headed into the garage.

Walking up the short flight of steps to the police station, Eliza stopped dead when three officers came rushing out the front doors. A fourth officer paused in the entrance when he saw Eliza and held the door open for her. "We're late getting our lunch," the man in uniform explained in recognition of the panicked look on Eliza's face. "I have the keys. They'll wait for me."

Eliza nodded in thanks to the officer and went into the lobby of the station. She moved past a line of chairs against the wall, some occupied, and some holding documents from the people next to them, and continued ahead to a window with a receptionist behind it. As Eliza approached, the window slid open slightly. "How can we help you today?"

"Chapel? Officer Chapel, please? He told me to come here to review some security—"

"Please wait in an available seat and we'll call your name." The bespeckled woman handed Eliza a clipboard with a paper containing a list of names. Upon recognition of the sign-in sheet, Eliza took the pen that was in the woman's other hand and scribbled her name in the appropriate box. As soon as the pen and clipboard were back through the window, it was slid shut by the gray-haired receptionist, who then pointed toward the chairs in the waiting area. Eliza's eyes followed the direction of the imaginary line between fingertip and wall and began walking along it.

The chairs already occupied gave Eliza pause. She scanned each person carefully, judging them only by their outward appearance, and trying to decide which was likely to be the safest one to sit near. Tattered jeans, messy tattoos, business suits, grimy hands, and missing shoes made up the costumes for the cast of characters. Focusing on the person whose hands looked like hers usually did, she noticed the generic white T-shirt they were wearing before realizing she recognized their face.

"Oh, shit. Eric," she said, approaching one of her fellow automotive shop owners. Her demeanor quickly lightened. "What're you in for?

The man looked up from the hole he was drilling into the floor with his eyes. His facial expression turned from stoic to thrill when he noticed who had addressed him. "Eliza? Damn. Don't tell me they hit your shop, too?"

"What? What happened? Why are you here?" She leaned down toward Eric.

"Someone ran off with one of my tool boxes. I was outside the shop, under the hood of a piece of junk trying to get a radiator out. I realized I left my grips in the garage, and when I came back out, my box was gone. I called the cops and they wanted me to come in to make a statement."

Eliza shook her head. "That sucks, man. Was it much? I have extras of some stuff if you need to borrow anything while you wait on replacements."

"No. Luckily this was my backup set. Just the easy stuff to carry in and out of the shop. But it was still a lot. I keep enough in there to tear down most of a car, you know."

"Right, yeah. Got it." Eliza took the seat next to Eric.

"So why are you here then?" Eric asked.

"Oh, uh, they just want me to watch some video for something that happened." Eliza pulled at the hair covering her right eye, making sure it was staying in place. "I had some free time."

"Free time? At your shop? You always seem busy," Eric joked. He knew about the videos Eliza posted online from her shop, and the extra business it had generated over the years. He wasn't too envious because occasionally she'd shout out his shop in her videos for some of his specialties. He was sure he had gained some new customers because of it.

"I try to build in a little open time here and there, but I wasn't expecting to use it today to be here."

"Same." He nodded. "Same."

"Eliza Banding?" boomed a voice from across the hall.

Standing up straight as if being called to the principal's office, Eliza turned to Eric. "Good luck getting your tools back, man. Maybe check the online sales sites? They might be dumb enough to try to sell them there."

"One can hope. Thanks, Eliza. I'll see you around." Eric stood while seeing her off.

Eliza headed in the direction of the voice to find a husky officer standing in the way of an open door. "Ms. Banding?" he asked, extending a hand to shake. With his other hand, he smoothed down each side of his bushy beard. "I'm Officer Chapel. Thanks for taking some time out of your day to come down. We're really sorry this happened to you." After Eliza reciprocated the handshake, the officer continued, "Follow me down the hall here and we'll get this out of the way so you can get back to work." With what seemed like an attempt to make some small talk while leading Eliza down the drab hallway of the building, Office Chapel asked, "What do you do for work, Ms. Banding?"

"Oh, uh, I own an auto body shop just outside of town here." Peering in the windows of the office doors as she passed, Eliza contemplated how much she wanted to share. "I've had it for about ten years now. I had lived here—down the street from here, actually—most of that time, but I recently moved, because, well . . ."

"Ah, yes, I understand. Again, I'm sorry that that happened to you. There's been an increase of crimes lately and we're trying our best to keep up." Officer Chapel stopped at an open doorway and gestured for Eliza to enter. "Please take a seat at the desk while I pull up the video on the computer. Unfortunately, we only have footage from inside the elevator. The apartment building doesn't have working cameras in the main hallways, so we don't know where the suspect came from, or where they were going. We're hoping that you recognize the person as a tenant of the complex."

Eliza uneasily adjusted herself in the wood-framed chair. The leather-like material let out a squeak every time she shifted her weight. While waiting for the officer to finish the awkward clicking of the trackpad on the laptop, his large hands nearly the size of the keyboard, she focused on a picture frame on his desk. In it was an image of a less-gray and less-bulky version of Officer Chapel, flanked by two young women who shared his facial features.

"Okay. Here we are, Ms. Banding." Officer Chapel turned the laptop around, showing a paused video of Eliza looking down at her phone while inside the elevator. He walked out from behind the desk and crouched next to Eliza. He groaned as his knees bent. "Are you ready to watch this? We can take another moment if you need it."

Eliza took a deep breath and turned to look at the side of the officer's head. She let out a quiet, "Yes. I'm ready."

After clicking the play button, Officer Chapel narrated the video as it proceeded. "The elevator doors open here and the suspect walks in. We don't get a good look at their face, but I'm hoping you recognize their clothing or another defining feature."

"No. Sorry," Eliza whispered.

The neatly-kept black hair of the man in the elevator obscured his face. He was wearing a form-fitting polo, dark blue jeans, and the white tips from his black Converse Chuck Taylor shoes looked new. "You don't recognize the shoes, Ms. Banding?" the officer asked.

"No. Half of the people in this area wear the same style shoes. I'm sorry."

The video continued to play. The points of the man's shoes began to turn in Eliza's direction. A nervous shift in the in-video Eliza's posture was more pronounced than the movement of the man. Her phone moved closer to her face. Present-day Eliza's posture mimicked that of her own on the screen. The man stepped forward and began to reach out a hand.

"Did he try to give you something, Ms. Banding?" Officer Chapel asked.

The deep voice startled Eliza, causing her to sit up straight. Through a whimper, she responded, "No. I don't think so. I didn't notice. I didn't see his hands."

The man in the video waved his hand low to the ground.

"Did he say anything to you?"

The suspense of the video kept Eliza from being able to speak, and she could only shake her head.

The hand stopped moving. A quick twitch of the fingers curling into a fist was almost overshadowed by the sudden movement the man made toward Eliza. Her body slammed against the side of the elevator when he pushed her against the wall. He stepped back and she slid downward, stunned. The side of her head hit the handrail.

Eliza shrieked.

The sound made the officer flinch, causing the palm of his hand to press down on the laptop's touchpad and pause the video. The picture on the screen showed the man with his hands up in the air, body leaned back, and his biceps protruding from his shirt sleeves. "Ahem." The officer cleared his throat in an attempt to cover up his own twitchiness. "There's only about thirty seconds left. Are you okay to continue?"

A timid nod from Eliza answered the officer.

The frames of the video started moving again, showing the attacker hopping and flailing his arms. A motionless Eliza laid on the ground while the man bent over. He rubbed his hands on his face and through his hair. The light in the elevator became more intense as the doors opened. Quickly jumping up, the man's dark hair fell forward over his eyes.

"Does the suspect look familiar here, Ms. Banding?"

"No. Still no," she whispered.

The man in the video glanced between the open doors and at Eliza on the ground. He walked out of the elevator, hugging the door frame. Less than a moment later, the first new passenger stepped on.

"That's Jan. Uh, Janet," Eliza said, unprompted.

"What was that, Ms. Banding?

"Janet."

"The one with her face down in her phone?" the officer asked. "Janet? Do you have a last name?"

"Um. Yes." Eliza had to switch gears and change her focus to the new question. "Lambert. Janet Lambert."

Scribbling down the name, Officer Chapel pointed at the screen when a new man walked into the elevator. The person's body language drastically changed as he noticed Eliza on the ground and kneeled beside her.

"Do you know him?" Officer Chapel asked.

"I've seen him around, but we've never spoken."

"Are you sure?"

Eliza nodded. "I don't know his name."

On screen, Eliza began to stir and rub at her head. She started backing away from the man crouching over her while he tried to calm her.

"Did he say anything to you?"

"He asked if I was okay. I—I don't know what else. I don't remember."

"Did he say if he saw who did it?"

"No."

Officer Chapel jotted down a few more notes as the video continued to run. Past-Eliza tried to stand before sitting down again.

"The building manager called an ambulance for me," Eliza said. "I went to the hospital. I had a gash on my eyebrow. It's just a bruise now." Her hand lightly pushed at a spot above her eye. "My coworker—my friend—came and picked me up."

"I'm glad it wasn't worse." The officer jotted down one more item in his notebook. "Is there anything else you would like to add, Ms. Banding?" Standing up, the officer towered over Eliza. He turned the laptop around and continued to his seat, waiting for her reply.

"No. No, that's all. I'm sorry."

"That's okay. You've been very helpful. Thank you for coming in, Ms. Banding." He pulled a business card from the top drawer of his desk and handed it to Eliza. "Please don't hesitate to reach out if you can think of anything else."

"I will. Thank you." Eliza stood.

"I'll be in touch if we need anything else," he said.

Eliza smiled timidly and left the office.

CHAPTER 11 - Eliza's Shop

"Oh, good. You're back," Allie said when Eliza returned to the shop. Oliver stood at the counter, holding his keys out to the receptionist. The two had been deep in conversation until Allie needed to cut it short when her boss walked through the door. "The owner of the Aston Martin is here and wants to talk to you."

Eliza nodded at Oliver then scanned the rest of the lobby. "Where?" she asked.

"Well, uh, he's in the garage." Allie scratched the back of her head.

Eliza glared at her.

"I know! You don't want anyone else in there when you're not. But he wanted to look over his car while he waited. He said he missed it. It's only been a couple minutes. I promise. And I can see him through the window. He hasn't moved."

With a chuckle, Eliza said, "I don't blame him. It's fine. I trust him." Turning to Oliver, Eliza changed topics. "I saw your car out there. Give me a second, all right?" She immediately left for the garage area.

"You got it," Oliver replied with a more playful tone than he had been using with Allie.

"*You got it*," she mimicked.

Oliver shot her a glare. "What?"

"I know she's cute, but she's got a date tomorrow, and it's a *second* one." Allie moved her focus to a box on the ground that she was stocking lobby shelves from and added, "You might have missed your chance."

"But I—"

"But nothing."

"Hey, Oli!" Eliza burst through the door, interrupting Oliver and Allie's conversation again and causing both to jump.

"Huh, what?" He acted innocent.

"I, uh, have to check over something with this guy." Eliza kept peering back over her shoulder in anticipation. "Just let Allie know what you need for your car—the wheel bearing, right?—and I'll try to get to it this afternoon. If you ask her nicely, she might be able to drive you back to the coffee shop."

"Okay, but, I wanted to ask if you think I should—"

"Great, thanks," Eliza said. She walked back through the door before Oliver could get another word out.

"No problem?" he replied.

Allie snorted, causing Oliver to face her.

"What?" he asked.

"Nothing. Let me finish up this box and I'll write up the work ticket for you."

"Do you want help?" He watched Allie continue emptying the box.

"Na. Because then you'd expect something for free."

"Didn't I just bring you and Eli a coffee?" He winked.

"True. Maybe I can convince her to write off the washer fluid."

"Thanks," he responded sarcastically.

"I'm done anyway." She kicked the empty cardboard box out of the way and went behind the desk to the computer. "So, sir," she began with feigned sincerity. "What would you like done today?" She licked the tip of an imaginary pen and then set her fingers on the shop computer's keyboard keys.

"The wheel bearing and a once-over. Oil, brakes . . . washer fluid? Make sure it's in working order. No hidden issues that I don't know about. I might be—"

"Allie," Eliza burst through the door again. "I'll be back, all right?"

"Sure, Boss."

Eliza disappeared back into the garage.

"Anyway, Oliver, *you* want the Eliza Special. Got it. Do you require a ride back to your home or place of business?" She wasn't hoping that the cute, well-built, scruffy man in front of her would say no, but she knew if he said yes, he would have to ride in her dirty beat-up car.

"I can walk back, Al. It's fine. And didn't Eli say she's leaving? I'd guess you should stay."

"Uh. Yeah. That's true. All right, well, we'll give you a ring when the car's done. Want us to use the coffee shop number or your phone?"

He handed his car key to Allie, before replying, "Either will work. Thanks. I'll see you later."

"You got it."

"Ha ha," he replied, recalling their earlier interaction. Oliver began walking to the exit before he paused.

"Forget something?" Allie asked.

He turned his head halfway to address Allie. "Does Eliza like Jeeps?"

"Sure. She'll work on anything with four wheels. Or two wheels. Or six wheels."

He nodded and continued on his way.

Spinning Oliver's key ring around her finger, Allie couldn't help herself from watching his backside as he walked out the door.

While standing in the parking lot, Oliver stared at an Aston Martin as it was pulling out of the furthest garage bay. He could see Eliza behind the wheel with a huge grin on her beautiful face. He sighed heavily while the car went past his parked Integra. After a dispirited look at his own vehicle, he said to himself, "Well, that makes up my mind."

"So, what do you think?" the owner of the Aston Martin Vantage F1 asked from the passenger seat.

Eliza kept both hands firmly planted on each side of the steering wheel of the supercar. "Oh. My. God. If I could afford one of these." She kept her eyes forward, knowing she would never forgive herself if she got into an accident. While the insurance she kept at her shop would cover the cost of the vehicle, her reputation with her customers would be tarnished, and she would be undoing the work she had recently completed on such a thing of beauty.

"Are you sure? I don't know, maybe I could cut you a good deal," he said.

"Like you would ever sell this." Eliza pulled up to a red light and activated the turn signal to head back to the shop.

"No. Not here. Keep going straight. Take it onto the highway. Open 'er up." The owner of the vehicle pointed at the entrance ramp to the interstate past the traffic light. "And, no, you're right. It took me a while to find this one. I think I'll keep it. Unless you want to trade me for that Supra of yours." A small chuckle left the man's mouth. "Put the windows down first. You'll want to hear it."

Eliza hesitated to respond, trying to deduce how her passenger knew she owned the Supra. With the blissful feeling of the steering wheel wrapped in her hands, she decided she didn't care. "If you're sure. You don't have anywhere to be? I have a couple more minutes before I should get back to work myself." She took a quick glance at the clock, realizing she had already taken up a portion of her day at the police station.

"I'm certain. Let's do it."

After putting the car windows down, a gust of wind blew through the cabin and pushed her hair back. She looked in the rearview mirror to check her surroundings and caught a glance of her right eye.

Ugh. Why's he looking at me? Her grip on the steering wheel tightened, knuckles turning white, and her eyes glazed over.

"Hey, you okay? The light's green," the man pointed out.

Shaking off the momentary flashback to the elevator, she looked up at the light. "Um, yeah, just checking that everyone stops before I go," she lied. "The people around here like to run right through these lights after they turn red."

"Ha. Right. Well, thanks for the caution. Now, hit the gas. See what she can do."

Easing around the bend of the on-ramp, Eliza began to straighten out the wheels. "You don't have to tell me twice," she said over the road noise. She checked the side mirror for the merge, then stomped down on the accelerator pedal, feeling the force of the sudden acceleration pushing her back in her seat. With the wind whipping through her hair, she remained focused on the road and the deep roar of the car's exhaust, not caring that the bruise on her face was uncovered, or what the man next to her might think. She was lost in the moment. Her grin was everything the car's owner had hoped for.

"Take the next exit and we can head back to your shop. You know, if you want," he said.

CHAPTER 12 - Him

He was once again following the Supra from E's Auto Body and Repair to Belinda's Brewpub. Rubbing his smooth cheeks and hairless upper lip with one hand while steering with the other, he was left pleased with his appearance as he pulled his car into the parking lot.

He regretted that he had missed spending the day sitting in the lot across from Eliza's shop, but he was happy that he had put the time into shaving and trimming other body hair. He had arrived in his preferred spot outside of her shop only fifteen minutes before she left for the day and was now parked at her favorite watering hole. He finally felt prepared to be near her.

She must really like this place. He wondered if he should tell her that it was one of his favorites. The thought of having to order a beer and drink it nauseated him. He hated the taste, no matter how hard he had tried. *Maybe I can convince her that I don't drive after I've been drinking.* His planning of what he would do if she offered to drive him home so he could have a beverage was interrupted when he saw her get out of her car and go into the building. She appeared to be in less of a hurry this time.

He was parked two rows back from Eliza's spot. It allowed him to walk past her Supra again, admiring its details up close, before he stopped to look in the tinted windows. He grinned at his own reflection. After bending down to rub at a dark spot on the white tips of his Chuck Taylors, he continued into the building, anxious about finding Eliza inside.

Upon opening the door, he cringed as the live music hit him. The raw sound scratched at the inside of his ears. He expected Eliza to want something more polished. Studio Music. Not *this*. He looked around the interior of the brewpub, easily spotting Eliza standing alone at a bar height table. Caught in a trance while watching her pick up a full pint glass, he focused on her lips pressing to the rim as she tilted her hand to bring the liquid to her mouth. He imagined what her lips would feel like pressed against his own. His tongue pushed past his teeth. He wanted to know how she tasted.

"Hey, bud," came a voice from behind him. "Can I get in?"

He realized he was still standing in the doorway, having never stepped a full foot into the building. Sliding out of the way for the man to go past, he never looked away from Eliza.

"Thanks," the voice said. "Nice shoes, by the way. The black version looks good."

His concentration was broken by the additional words. He looked at the person who addressed him, and then down at his own feet before noticing the man's nearly matching footwear. "I— thanks." The words fell on deaf ears as the man continued straight past and stopped at the same table where Eliza was standing.

"Who the hell is that?" he growled. His demeanor shifted suddenly. He barely kept the words to a volume that only he could hear. *Is she smiling? It looks like she's smiling.*

Finally stepping fully into the bar, he eyed an open booth near Eliza and the man who joined her. With his focus on Eliza's guest, he tried drilling a hole through the man's head with his eyes while he moved toward the table. When the person didn't drop dead, he felt dejected. He sat with an ear turned toward the two.

"Thanks again for the reschedule," he heard Eliza's date say. "I finished up the project for that client I mentioned. You know, the one with a boatload of money. That bonus should be pretty sweet when it shows up. I might have to get myself a new watch or a set of gold cufflinks. I already have a pair, of course, but it can't hurt to have a backup."

Out of the corner of his eye, he noticed Eliza pick up her pint glass to take a large sip and roll her eyes at the same time. The audible laugh that slipped out from his mouth made him concerned that the focus would shift to him, so he briefly turned his back to Eliza's table.

A server approached as he prepared to return to eavesdropping on the conversation a table over.

"What can I get you?" they asked.

Anxious for the interruption to end, he replied, "Just surprise me."

"You know, we actually hate when people tell us that," the server said. "We'll gladly offer up suggestions, if we know what to work with. Do you like beer? What kind of beer? Or do you like whiskey? Or how about a cocktail? We don't actually make many of those here, being a brewpub and all, but I guess we could figure it out." The waiter pulled out a small notepad and readied their pen for his response.

The person's attempt at small talk was making it hard to hear Eliza's side of the conversation. A wish for the server to be quiet and leave caused him to unintentionally respond with a stern, "Beer."

His attitude was masked by the cymbal splash from the band in the corner. The server asked several rapid-fire follow-up questions. "Great. What kind? IPA? Stout? We make good stouts. Wheat?"

"Wheat." The abruptness was again covered up by the drummer. He gagged slightly when he realized what he requested, but the feeling was quickly alleviated when it seemed to have finished the conversation with the server.

"Okay, I'll be right back with that." The employee put their pen away without writing anything and left to get the beverage.

With his focus once again on Eliza and her date's conversation, he noticed that the man was still talking about himself.

"And then after I got my MBA, I realized how much I love working with money. And you know, having money."

He couldn't tell if Eliza's date was intentionally fidgeting with his wallet that was sitting on the pub table next to his phone and keys. The man's fingers repeatedly slid out each of the credit cards halfway and then pushed them back in. Maybe it was a nervous habit, or maybe he was a narcissist.

"So, tell me about yourself," the date said. "Lindsay says you own your own business. I bet I could help you with your portfolio."

The thought of finally hearing Eliza's voice excited him. He wanted her to talk about herself so he could learn more details about her life, but he was left sorely disappointed when the man immediately continued with, "I like what you're wearing, by the way. I had to figure out what to wear to a place like this. I stopped by the store on the way over, you know, after realizing what I had on the other night was a little overdone. I figured I'd fit in just fine with these."

He followed the man's line of sight down to the pristine pair of tan Chuck Taylors he was wearing. The sales tag was still attached and tucked into the side.

"Yeah. I, uh—" Eliza began.

Watching Eliza peer around the table to follow her date's gaze down to the footwear, he audibly laughed a second time when Eliza picked up the pint glass from the table and took a drink, turning her head and shaking it just enough for him to notice.

Mine are at least authentic, he thought to himself. *I didn't just go buy them today to try and fit in. And black is better.*

A noticeable silence between Eliza and the man with her left him hopeful that she would finally get a chance to speak. He was elated when she did.

"Yes. I own my own business," she said. "It's an auto body shop. Just on the outside of town here. I change oil and—"

"*You're* a mechanic?" Her date didn't hide his surprise. "Lindsay never mentioned that."

Hardly keeping his opinion inside his head, he thought, *Yes she is, you jerk. You*—

The idea was interrupted when Eliza answered, "I am, yes. I love it. But I do more than that there. Besides taking care of the different vehicles that come in, I have to order the products for the shop, which my assistant helps immensely with, and keep the business running. I'm generally the only mechanic at my shop, but sometimes I'll bring in someone else while they're trying to learn. Mentor them."

"Mentor them? So, you're not getting paid when training them? Wouldn't you want to make as much as you—"

"I'm still getting paid. The customer still has their vehicle in the shop."

He could hear her annoyance.

"But you could have the trainee pay, too," Eliza's date said. "Like a trade school. Get a double dipping of that—"

"No. I don't do that. Someone helped me get started, so the least I can do is help someone else."

Eliza cutting off the man for a second time caused the curl on each side of his mouth to hit unnatural heights. If he wasn't listening intently before, he was now.

"Whatever," the man with Eliza replied.

Whatever? Whatever? he thought. *What the hell kind of answer is that? You don't whatever her. I'll whatever you if you ever—* He couldn't figure out how to finish the threat before he noticed Eliza had stopped talking. *No, don't stop. Please. I want to hear more.* He was relieved when he heard her voice again, until his server showed up and stood between his table and Eliza's.

"So sorry for the wait. We got about a half pour of the wheat for you when the keg kicked. Then we had to pull up a new keg from the basement. But someone had moved the hand truck. Once we found that, we could get the keg. And then we hooked it up, but the seal just wouldn't hold. It kept leaking, making a mess all over the place. Either way, here's your drink. Sorry again. This one's on me."

Staring up at the server with frustration, he could only get out a faint, "Okay." When he noticed that the person who brought out the drink was still standing there, he tried to think on his feet to find a way to get them to leave. "Thanks?"

"Hey, you got it. Just grab my attention if you need anything else. Yeah?"

"Sure?"

"The band is taking a break too, but they'll be back on shortly."

"Great."

"I'll check on you later."

"Thanks."

He was relieved when the server finally turned away, but that feeling was fleeting when all they did was turn to Eliza's table.

"Do either of you two love birds need anything else?"

A seething anger bubbled up at the thought of Eliza being with someone other than himself. Seeing the man with Eliza was one thing, but putting a term to it was another. He started to stand. He wanted to reach out and grab the waiter, throw them on the ground, and kick them until they stopped moving. He would immediately grab Eliza's date to do the same. After, he'd polish any red splotches off of the tips of his shoes. The anger quickly subsided when he heard Eliza spit out the drink in her mouth. The splattering of the liquid as it hit the ground didn't disgust him, but rather he had to hold back true laughter at the real-life spit-take he had witnessed.

"Oh, ew. What was—ew. I'm— I'm going to go, uh, powder my nose," the man with Eliza said. He immediately headed off in the direction of the restrooms while holding his hands up in revulsion.

"I'm so sorry about that," Eliza offered the server. "That was not intended. We're definitely not together."

"No worries, deary. My mistake for assuming." The server pulled a wad of napkins out of their pocket and began to lean down toward the floor.

Eliza stopped the server and took the napkins to clean up the mess herself, leaving him awestruck. He tried to will himself to get up from his seat and help her, too. The struggle to find the words he would use once eye-to-eye with her created an internal tug of war. After finally putting his first foot down on the ground to help, he was stopped in his tracks when the voice of her date returned.

"When you're done with that, do you want to head somewhere else?" the man asked.

A burning rage rose up again. *She wouldn't go somewhere with him. Right? She can't be into someone like that. Can she?* Questioning himself with everything he thought he was so sure of, he found himself answering for Eliza.

"No."

"I'm sorry, what?" the man asked Eliza. He towered over her while she finished wiping up the last wet spot.

"I said, no," she replied.

"Well, why not? I thought we were having fun." Her date placed both of his hands on his hips and continued to look down at Eliza.

He couldn't hear exactly what Eliza had said under her breath, but imagined that it sounded something like, "That's one of us." His anger subsided as another wave of relief washed over him.

"I have work I need to do," she said at full volume. "I should get going."

"Fine, I'm going to head out then. I'll call you to get you on my calendar."

"Please don't," was what he thought he heard Eliza say, but the other man didn't seem to notice as he turned to leave the brewpub.

Eliza started to rise from the floor where she had left a large clean spot. His attention was on her date as he walked out the door. He decided it was time for him to go, too. He knew he could check in on Eliza when she finished at the shop tomorrow, but for now, he wanted to make sure she didn't have to deal with an asshole like the person who just walked out on her.

He rushed out the exit, trying to find the man that left.

"Did you not like the wheat beer?" he heard the server trying to ask as the door swung shut behind him.

Out in the parking lot, he was focused on finding the man who left Eliza. "What symbol was on the car key?" he asked himself. He knew he saw it. "Mercedes, Volvo, BMW? No, it didn't have those colors." He scanned the parking lot and saw a set of headlights light up. "Buick. That's it." Hurrying to his own car, he slid into the driver seat and started the engine. He quickly pulled through the open spot in front of him and crept forward, waiting for the other car to turn onto the street.

They were the only two cars on the secluded single lane road, making it easy to track the man's movements, even in the dim light of the night. The taillights remained directly ahead of him as his mind raced. He followed the vehicle through several street lights until it dawned on him that he didn't know what he would do if he were to catch his prey. Would he confront Eliza's date? Would he call him an asshole to his face? *No, I can't do that,* he answered himself. He started to let the car in front of him gain extra ground until its taillights were barely visible. With his motel only a few turns back, he decided that he would much rather spend the rest of the night rewatching Eliza's videos. Hearing her voice without the extra background noise and music in the brewpub sounded smarter. He changed his course, happier with his new plan.

CHAPTER 13 - Always Working

What a shit date, Eliza thought to herself as she walked through the door of her apartment. *What a stuck-up, pompous ass. And thinking I'd want to see him a third time?* She recalled the smug look he had while he was standing over her as she cleaned the bar floor. It was almost his fault to begin with, yet he assumed that she'd want another date. "Ass," she said out loud finally.

"How am I going to let Lindsay know? She's gotta deal with him at work—he's not my type—that'll work. He's definitely not. Probably doesn't even know a tailpipe from his own cock. Though he might be dumb enough to try to fuck one, even if it's hot." She shuddered at the thought as the image appeared in her mind.

Having already removed her shoes, she didn't wait to make it into the bedroom before taking off her shirt and unbuttoning her pants. Eliza felt dirty having worn those clothes around that man. She glanced at the open blinds for her balcony, thankful that she hadn't turned on the light when she walked in. Across the courtyard, she could clearly see into the opposite apartment where two young boys were running around and throwing pillows at each other.

"Almost gave them a show," Eliza said with a chuckle.

She pulled the blinds shut for the night, then went to her bedroom to continue disrobing.

Eliza hoped that she could salvage the rest of the night by being productive. She slid into her bed and grabbed the laptop off of the nightstand, placing it on her bare legs. The cold metal frame of the thin computer made her momentarily shiver until she adjusted to the temperature difference. Shortly after turning on the device, it warmed up, providing a more comfortable feeling.

Eliza opened the editing software she used for her videos. She found the file for the recent PPF job she performed and stared at the first frame. An image of a freshly cleaned Aston Martin stared back at her. She began scanning through the video. Watching the preview frames quickly change, she looked for the point in time where she picked up the camera to move it for different shots. She made a mental note to buy another camera after recalling that her secondary recording device was crushed when a tire unexpectedly tipped over. Having the additional camera allowed her to splice in clips of other viewpoints without having to edit out the unnecessary video when limited to one device. Once she found the location that she was looking for, she selected the portion of the video that included the camera movement, and several frames past, to be removed. After hitting the delete key on the keyboard, she looked off beyond the screen, giving her eyes a break.

The fan of the laptop spun up as the computer was performing the laborious task. The gentle vibration through her legs gave her a brief moment of pleasure on her thighs, sore from the day's work. She thought about Allie's comment about the computer at the shop. Eliza knew that it wouldn't be able to handle this kind of processor-intensive work, but she still thought it would be able to survive another year or two of keeping inventory for her business and allowing Allie to ring up customers. When it could no longer perform those tasks, then it would need to be replaced.

The thought of spending money briefly brought her back to her date. She again said, "Ass," out loud almost as soon as the laptop finished its work; like a vulgar *ding* as a reward for being finished.

Eliza set the position of the video to just prior to the camera location change and hit play. She made sure that the cutover was smooth and didn't include any of the audio commentary to herself. Hearing a couple clicks and clunks, but overall happy with the video, she selected a small section and set the volume for the audio to zero.

Eliza returned to scanning through the video frames, remembering that she moved the camera not too long after the first time. When she found what she was looking for, she repeated the process of removing the unnecessary frames, playing back the new edit, and removing the audio pops and clicks. The playback bar in the editor showed that she still had forty minutes of video left to review. She peeked at the clock and was grateful that it wasn't as late as she had feared. She only drank one beer at the brewpub, not wanting to risk driving under the influence, so she set the laptop aside and headed to the kitchen.

While walking, she rubbed at her legs, now free from the weight of the computer, and stretched the rest of her limbs. After opening the refrigerator door, she pulled a can out of the recently purchased four-pack of IPAs and lifted the pull tab. The spritz from the carbonated beverage hit her hand. She used her barely covered backside to wipe off the drips. Eliza took a quick sip before returning to her bedroom with the can in hand.

Setting the drink on the nightstand beside her, she returned to her bed and set the laptop back on her lap. Eliza braced herself for another cold shock, forgetting that the computer had been running for an extended time. The warm bottom touched her legs, leaving her gratified at the new temperature difference.

Eliza continued scanning through the video, looking for any frames that seemed to be out of place, while watching the quickened pace of herself laying the PPF on the super car. She hit the play button at the point where she was squeegeeing out the tack solution, and turned up the volume on the computer so she could hear it clearly. She had become accustomed to recordings of herself and found her own voice to be pleasant. Eliza continued listening to make sure she didn't have any slip-ups in the terminology used and that she was enunciating clearly. While she wouldn't be able to rerecord any of the steps, she could at least put subtext on the screen to clear up any confusion.

Eliza reached for the beer can on her nightstand and took a sip while closing her eyes to listen intently to the audio of the tutorial video. Happy with the progress, she blindly reached down to the keyboard and tapped the spacebar to pause the playing content. She moved her hand, finding the left and right arrow keys, and pressed the key to skip further ahead.

She began the video again while taking another drink of her beverage. Eliza concentrated on the final step, and her quick request for anyone watching the video to *like and subscribe*. She opened her eyes to watch the final scene where she reached out to the camera to stop the recording session. She selected the final few frames in the video editing software and hit the delete key. With her eyes closed again, the laptop fan spun up fast enough to cause a gentle hum through the base of the computer.

The sound of the vibration caused her mind to wander. She cracked open an eye and glanced toward her dresser drawer, contemplating replacing one battery-powered device with another. She was disappointed when the software was done with its task and the fan of the laptop wound back down, not giving her enough time to set the device aside.

Eliza considered selecting a much larger group of frames in the video to delete, hoping for a longer duration that the computer would be tied up, and an excuse to put it aside. At the risk of the *Undo* button failing her, she decided to save the progress and close the video, moving onto the next step.

Eliza opened the folder that contained her various recorded tutorials and do-it-yourself videos. She looked inside the subfolder that held her published works. With a glance at the bottom of the newly opened window, she found the count indicating how many videos she had shared with her followers. The number 123 was displayed, causing her to grin slightly at the sequential listing. She mentally counted the number of days before her planned live stream event. A realization hit her of how much she would personally enjoy making the live stream be her one hundred and twenty-fifth published video. She backed out to the full list of video files and found the unpublished, but fully edited and ready, folder of files. She picked one to immediately put online.

The video showed her buffing out a scratch on the driver side door of a Range Rover and blending in the touch-up paint. She thought that it might be cheating slightly, picking one of her shorter videos for the one hundred and twenty-fourth, but she opened the website she used to upload her files and dragged the video to the box anyway. She typed a short message in the description field.

I know this one is coming a little early, but surprise! Just wait until the next video. The live stream from E's Auto Body and Repair.

Happy with the text on the screen of her laptop, she clicked the *Publish when Ready* button.

While waiting for the streaming platform hosting her videos to do its part in processing the new file, Eliza opened the page for the published video of her laying red PPF on her own Supra to do some housekeeping. In an attempt to mentally prepare herself for the barrage of typically unhelpful, pointless, and at times vulgar and repulsive comments, she picked up her beer can and shook it lightly side-to-side. The sloshing indicated that there was about half left. She readied her other hand over the delete key. After taking a long swig, Eliza began to read the comments.

He clicked the bookmark in his computer browser that was labeled with the default name provided from when he created it years ago. The *E's Auto Body and Repair: Videos* webpage loaded on the screen. Two new videos he had not yet watched were sitting at the top. He slammed his fist into the cushion of the dingy motel room couch. The hat sitting next to him was swatted away while he wondered how he had missed the release of a second video. Eliza was very consistent with how often she shared herself with him. He was frustrated being behind.

His mood quickly changed when he realized that his next couple of hours would be spent watching, and rewatching each video, trying to gain further insight into Eliza's mind. He would continue to learn her mannerisms and interests, so that he would be even more prepared to have the in-person conversation that he had been waiting for.

Choosing the video with the thumbnail showing a completely white Supra, he made himself as comfortable as he could. The springs from the couch poked him in weird places with each shift. He crossed and uncrossed his legs while holding up the laptop, eventually moving to the middle of the couch and splitting his weight between the two cushions. Finally settled, he placed the laptop down, and adjusted the volume to a setting that would be loud enough to hear every word Eliza said without distorting the soothing voice he had become accustomed to. He pressed play and closed his eyes.

A full-body, tingling sensation shot through him as Eliza addressed him.

"Welcome to another video from E's Auto Body and Repair."

He tilted his head back while he imagined her in the room with him.

"Today we're working on—"

There was a slight audio pop that jolted him. He opened his eyes as the on-screen Eliza continued talking.

"A Supra."

He went back several seconds in the video and started it again.

"Today we're working on—*click*—a Supra."

He paused the video and opened a folder on his computer labeled *Eliza*. He created a new file to add to the other one hundred and twenty-two text documents already present. Each was labeled by date and an associated vehicle. To name the new file, he added the current date followed by a dash and the word *Supra*. After opening the blank document, he began typing.

0:00:05 Audio pop before Eliza mentions the Supra. Possible video edit.

Bringing the browser window to the forefront again, he hit play and closed his eyes to listen.

After Eliza requested that he *like and subscribe*—something he had done years prior—the remainder of the audio in the video was complete. He brought the text file to the foreground and added one more note at the end of a list that had grown to twenty distinct comments about what he heard.

1:00:07 Smooth audio fadeout.

If he had found himself sitting with Eliza in the next moment, he would easily be able to repeat the content of the video. There would be no question from her that he understood what she told him. Even with mistakes in the audio, he would blame the technology. Everything about Eliza was perfect. He kept these notes with hopes to show her that his attention to small details could match hers.

He returned to the browser window and clicked on the replay button that was now showing over a black background. He rubbed his eyes and focused on the screen as the video began to play. Turning the volume down slightly, he studied the moving images as he listened with half an ear as Eliza stared back from the computer.

"Today we're working on a Supra," she said to him.

Once more switching to the text file, he added a note to the end of the very first line he had created about the audio pop.

No obvious video inconsistency.

Perfect, he thought. *Of course that glitch wasn't her fault.* The video had been left running. He started it over, afraid he may have missed something.

At the halfway point, he began to realize what he was seeing. He was so focused on the audio quality and edits during his listen-through that he never caught Eliza's mention of the color red. While watching her pick up a sheet of red PPF and place it on the trunk lid of the Supra, his eyes widened. He couldn't contain his excitement. He scanned further ahead in the video, something he never did. Eliza moved at lightning speed to change the back of the car, *her* car, from white to red. He had seen the Supra in person. He knew the car, but had thought that Eliza never shared her own vehicle with him before. The all-white Supra in her previous videos must have been her own. Not just another customer vehicle.

He wanted to get Eliza's attention. He opened the comment box under the video and typed a short message.

You have a nice Supra.

He thought back to the messages he had posted on Eliza's older videos. Each contained little more than a smiley face, a thumbs up, or occasionally the word *nice*. He re-read the text typed in the box. Five simple words. He made sure each was spelled correctly, that they were in the right order, and that the capitalization was perfect. His anxiety spiked momentarily when he thought he had forgotten to type an uppercase S for the word Supra. He believed that Eliza would never forgive him for mistyping such an important word with the attention to detail that she exhibited. Wavering back and forth between using the closing period or an exclamation point, he read the words one more time and decided to leave them as they were. He clicked the button to submit the comment and shut the laptop lid in embarrassment.

CHAPTER 14 - They Start Packing

"So, it's settled, Johnny?" Lindsay began. "We're leaving for the cabin this weekend?"

"Booked and ready," he shouted from the kitchen, his head in the oven while pulling out the freshly baked chicken cordon bleu.

"I guess we should start packing then," Lindsay said. She appeared in the entry of the room and cocked her head to stare at her husband while he was still bent over. His long blonde hair was hanging off to the side.

Johnny turned around to find his wife's line of sight down below his waist and sucked in his gut.

"What are you doing?" she asked in return.

"Making myself look good." He patted his stomach. "I guess I should have spent the last week working out to get in shape for our trip."

"John, you never stop moving. You're on your feet all day every day at your job sites. And for ten hours some days. So, shut up."

"Moooommy." Nilah popped up from behind the kitchen island with her hands on her hips.

"I know, baby. Mommy shouldn't have told Daddy to—" Lindsay looked Johnny straight in the eyes. "Shut up." She blew him a kiss, then asked, "Need help with anything?"

"Ni's drink is in the fridge, but I think everything else is ready." Distributing the food out to the plates in front of him, Johnny returned the conversation back to their trip. "Eliza's got to get back over here to get my car. We want to leave Friday afternoon, right?"

"You tell me." Lindsay took Nilah's plate and began cutting up the piece of chicken sitting on it. "When's check-in?"

"Four. Should take us about three hours to get there. Not that we need to be on time." Johnny thought about the last time they went to the cabin, before Nilah was born, and how the three-hour drive took them almost six because of different sightseeing stops they made on the way. "Maybe we should give ourselves a little bit more time, though. I know you don't want to miss the cookies that they put out."

Lindsay didn't have time to stop the words coming out of Johnny's mouth, knowing what the immediate reaction from their young daughter would be.

"I want a cookie!"

Looking up and taking in a deep breath, Lindsay spoke to Nilah. "If you eat your dinner, including your green beans, maybe you can have a cookie for dessert."

Johnny looked toward Lindsay and silently mouthed *Sorry*.

After counting back in her head from arrival time at the cabin to the time they needed to leave their house, Lindsay asked Johnny, "And you're sure Eliza can get Ni around noon?"

"She swore she could. I'm not sure what she's going to do about the shop, but it is a Friday and it is her shop. She has Allie to ring up customers, and I guess if she had to, she could take Ni back with her. We'll send her with some coloring books."

"And her tablet," Lindsay added.

"And her tablet," he agreed.

Prodding Nilah along to eat her dinner, the thought of leaving her daughter began to worry Lindsay. She knew Eliza was more than responsible enough and cared a great deal for her niece, but she was still concerned about being away from Nilah for even a couple of days.

"I see the worry lines on your face, Linds. It'll be okay," he reassured his wife. "I pulled out the sleeping bag for Ni to take with her. But we'll have to pack her stuffed piggy the day we leave." He knew how many times Nilah would call out for her stuffed animal in the middle of the night if they dared to pack it early. But if he didn't say something out loud about it now, there was no hope that either he or

Lindsay would remember it. Otherwise, Nilah wouldn't know it was missing until being tucked into bed at Eliza's.

"I know it'll be okay. I'm still going to worry." Trying to push the thoughts to the back of her mind, she thought of everything that Nilah would need for her time with her aunt, and how packing for the young girl would require just as much effort as packing for vacation for herself. "Ni, after dinner, let's pick out some books you can take to Aunt Eliza's house. We can pick a couple that you can read to her, okay? And you can bring some that maybe she'll read to you?"

"My piggy book that came with my stuffie!" Nilah agreed. "Aunt 'liza can read that to me."

"You can read that one yourself."

"Yes, but Aunt 'liza can read it, too."

Seeing that the conversation about the books wasn't going to move forward, Lindsay again pushed Nilah to finish her dinner with the bribe of dessert. "Eat two more bites, please."

"I'm not hungry."

"Do you still want a cookie?" the girl's mother asked, knowing the answer without needing a response.

Nilah put two bites worth of food into her mouth at once and mumbled, "Yes."

After a heavy sigh, Lindsay got up and went toward the pantry. She pulled out a package of cookies and first offered them to Johnny. "John, do you want one?"

He shook his head and patted his belly. With his fork, he stabbed the green beans still on Nilah's plate. After loading the prongs full, he shoved the vegetables into his mouth.

Lindsay took the hint and ate the first cookie before placing one on Nilah's plate. "John, are the suitcases out yet?"

"Not yet. I'll grab them after we're done. Can we get away with just one?" He chuckled before adding, "Will any more than that even fit in your trunk?"

"The trunk can't be that much smaller than my old car," she answered. "But I can probably fit all of my stuff into the big suitcase."

"And my clothes?" Johnny responded. He knew that his wife's reply would be a joke at his expense, but he was curious what the remark would be.

"You'll be wearing clothes there, right? What more do you need?"

Left impressed with the comment, he couldn't get out any of the responses he had prepared as a possible retort. "Right. Yup. Right."

Lindsay took the win and returned her focus to her daughter. "Nilah, how long does it take to eat a cookie? It'll be time for bed once you're finally done." Watching Johnny take his and Nilah's empty plates and load them into the dishwasher, Lindsay thought about packing again, knowing that she wouldn't actually need to take much with her. "How's the weather out there this weekend? Will I need long pants?"

"You probably won't need any pants," Johnny responded deadpan, trying to hide the purpose behind the response from his daughter's prying ears.

"Johnny!" Lindsay yelled at him anyway.

"I'm checking, I'm checking," he promised. After washing his hands, he briefly looked at the weather on his phone. "Warm enough to not need long pants. Some rain on the day we'll come home. Not bad otherwise."

"Thank you. No pants it is," Lindsay replied. She was happy that her husband didn't provide any additional innuendos around their young daughter, but was unable to keep herself from playing along. Realizing the mistake, she quickly added, "Maybe a dress."

Johnny smirked, pleased to have his wife on the same page, then noticed Nilah was still sitting at the kitchen table finishing her dessert. "Ni, come on. Go wash your hands and then you can help me get the stuff we all need for our trips."

Nilah shoved the rest of the cookie into her mouth. A barely coherent, "Okay," came from her as she sprinted to the bathroom.

Happy with himself for getting Nilah to finally leave the kitchen, he said to Lindsay, "She just needed some encouragement. I'll get the luggage out and we can start packing. At least we still have a few days."

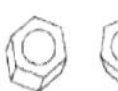

"Ms. Banding," the man on the other end of the phone call said as Eliza was preparing her dinner.

"Officer Chapel?" she responded, recognizing the number on the phone as the one he used previously when calling her.

"Yes, Ms. Banding. I hope you are having a good evening."

The deep voice paused, waiting for a response to the pleasantries before continuing on with the purpose of the call.

"Yes, Officer." Eliza waited anxiously for what she hoped was an update regarding the person who had attacked her in the elevator. The long moment in between gave her enough time to picture the four walls of the small space around her and the white tips of the Chuck Taylors that were visible past the top of her phone screen.

"I wish I was calling with some better news."

Another pause and Eliza was looking up from the floor of the elevator, through the faces asking her if she was okay, and at the fluorescent lights.

"Unfortunately, we don't have any leads in discovering who attacked you or why. We've been unable to speak with everyone in the apartment complex, but we hope someone will come forward soon with some information." The gap for a response from Eliza was closed quicker this time with a new question posed to her. "Have you been able to remember anything else, Ms. Banding?"

"I don't— No. Sorry. No." Eliza wasn't prepared for the question. She was sure she answered it correctly, however. She repeated the response just in case. "No. Nothing."

"Just as well, Ms. Banding. I will be in touch if we find anything. Please do have a good evening."

"You too?" Not meaning to pose the response as a question, she hung up the phone rather than trying to correct herself.

"Dammit!" she shouted, watching as water boiled over the pot on the stovetop. "There goes my worry-free night."

CHAPTER 15 - Dad

25 Years Prior

"Eliza Melissa Banding, hold that flashlight steady."

"But, Dad, it's Johnny's turn." The heavy stainless steel flashlight weighed down a young Eliza's arms while she gripped it tightly in both hands. The old pickup truck that her father was working on in the dusk offered no place to use for additional leverage.

"John will get his turn, but right now I want *you* to watch what I'm doing here." Eliza's father took a metal pipe, left over from an old chain link fence that used to enclose the backyard of their property, and stuck an open end over the socket wrench hanging off of a nut on the passenger side tie rod. "I want you to know how to do this. I'm not always going to be around, and with your mother gone, and me not really being able to teach you how to prune petunias, or anything else that she liked to do before—"

"Dad, I don't want to talk about—" Eliza tried to stop her father from finishing his sentence. The loss of her mother, and his wife of nearly two decades, still put a heavy weight on the happenings around the house.

"Eliza, let me finish. I can't teach you everything. I can teach you a lot, but there were just some things that she was much better at, and hopefully you and your brother were able to pick up some of that." He stopped and cleared his throat, an attempt to cover up a sniffle that Eliza noticed. "Damn bugs." One additional throat-clearing allowed him to continue. "But I can teach you how to diagnose and fix almost any problem with a car."

"This is a truck, Dad." She couldn't help herself from ribbing on her father, even during sentimental times like this.

"Or truck, miss stubborn. You definitely got your mother's humor." Eliza's father pulled the newly extended socket wrench toward himself. He started speaking again as if he had never stopped to discuss the missing family member. His audience needed to know how to break loose a stuck nut. "So, we sprayed this sucker with some lubricating oil, let it soak for a while, and now we put this pipe on here for some additional leverage. If that doesn't get it turning, I don't know what will." He pulled hard and the makeshift breaker bar easily moved the nut a half-rotation. "See, painless. Now, Eliza," he said, directing his attention to the singular viewer of his tutorial. "Give me the flashlight. I want you to get that nut the rest of the way off."

Eliza handed the flashlight to her father, happy to be rid of the physical weight, but still holding onto the emotional baggage, and crouched down into the wheel well of the vehicle. At her father's guidance, she pulled off the pipe extending the wrench, placed it gently on the ground, then grabbed onto the shortened socket wrench. The clicking of the tool, which caused a small vibration up her arms when she pushed the wrench away from herself, was a familiar sound. One she heard often from the side yard of their house when her father was not inside. She pulled the lever toward herself and it easily moved. She repeated the process. Several clicks followed by a pull, until the opposite end of the wrench dropped. The nut fell, rolling away. Eliza lunged, making sure it didn't get out of reach. The thunk of her shoulder into a bare lug bolt had her pause and rub at the impending bruise while she held tight to the mutineering nut.

"And that, Eliza, is why you should find a job that pays you enough so you don't have to do this yourself. Pay someone like me to do it instead. A degree in economics might work." Eliza's father crouched down next to her and held the beam of the flashlight over the injury that she exposed after pulling her shirt sleeve above her shoulder. "Didn't even break the skin. You'll be fine."

"But, Dad, what if this *is* what I want to do?" Her scrunched face failed to hide the pain that she was still trying to rub away. "Don't people pay to get their cars fixed?"

"Hey," he started, meeting her eyes. "Just find something that you like doing. Hell, find something you *love* doing. I just want you to be happy. Okay?"

Eliza nodded. The awkwardness of her father showing emotion over the last fifteen minutes of hard labor rendered her speechless.

"And someday, you'll be able to teach a little kid of your own. Maybe a boy, maybe a girl, but you'll know how to do it." Eliza's father abruptly turned his head and shouted, "John! Get over here. It's your turn."

Eliza grinned at hearing her father's stern, rugged voice. *That's more like it*, she thought.

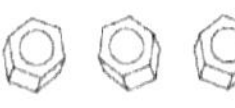

Present Time

"And that, folks, is how we replace a tie rod on an early model year F-150. If I did anything wrong . . ." Eliza looked up and closed her eyes tight. "My father will be sure to let me know. Somehow." She returned her focus to the camera in front of her. "Until next time, I'm Eliza at E's Auto Body and Repair, right at the corner of West Victoria and Chestnut."

Eliza reached over to the camera and shut it off. She wiped at the corner of her eye, expecting to find it wet. She hoped that any tears she did release could be easily edited out and the sniffles could be panned down without messing with the other audio on her recording.

CHAPTER 16 - Still Working

"You have a nice Supra." Eliza read the words out loud from the computer screen. The comment was displayed under the preview image for the video of her Supra and next to a profile picture showing a silver SUV.

"You? I? They can't know that it's mine. I'm so careful about that. I even edited out the video when I said *my Supra*." Eliza thought hard. She remembered telling her future self that she needed to remove it when recording the video, but she couldn't remember if she actually did. Rewatching her own videos after they were already published wasn't something that she had time for.

She took a deep breath. "My best customers all know my car." Eliza relaxed slightly, feeling her heartbeat begin to slow. "It has to be one of them." She didn't recognize the car in the profile picture. Over the course of a month, let alone the last several years, she saw many nondescript vehicles come through her shop. Allie handled most of the customer interactions, so it could just be one of her oil change and air filter replacement regulars. Questioning her paranoia, she hit the button next to the comment indicating that she approved of the message and moved on to the next comment.

Eliza immediately placed the mouse cursor near the delete icon, knowing that she typically had to clear out several responses related to where the watcher would like to place their dipstick. If it wasn't a comment about her looks, it was how women—though the commenter generally used more colorful terms—didn't know how to work on cars. Eliza usually found some humor in these statements when the picture attached to the comment was of a vehicle that was lucky to start on the first try, if ever at all.

Surprised to find an actual question left to her in the list of messages, Eliza paused to think how best to respond. "How did I make sure that the diagonal line on both sides of the car, splitting the red and the white, were symmetrical?" She thought back to using her tape measure, a dry erase marker, and a lot of patience, and began typing.

I did a lot of the prep for where I wanted to lay the wrap prior to recording the video. Next time I'll make sure to include that part. But to answer your question, I busted out my trusty tape measure and used a dry erase marker (yes, you read that correctly), to mark where I wanted the angle for the PPF to follow. If you watch the video again, you might be able to see a couple marks toward the midpoint of the car. I use red markers because they clean up easier, and if you slip and get it on any of the rubber gaskets, you can hardly see it. It's so light. After laying the wrap, just use some rubbing alcohol to get any visible markings off.

After posting the response, she finished going through the rest of the messages on the video of her Supra, and checked the remainder of her notifications. A grouping of comments from one particular user showed several single smiley faces and a few thumbs ups. Eliza hit the button to clear the notification indicator and decided she'd had enough of her computer screen for the night. Once the lid was closed and the laptop placed on the nightstand, she grabbed the beer can and took the last swig. She climbed out of her bed to get ready to go to sleep. Before making it to her bathroom to clean up, Eliza shuffled her feet across the carpeted floor on her bare feet until she ended at the small tiled section at the front door. She put her face up to the door, closing her right eye and looking through the peephole with the other. The white glow from the front of her car under the apartment parking lot lights made her grin.

"I do have a nice Supra."

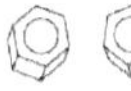

The ding from the laptop sitting next to him on his couch was louder than the background noise from the TV he was using to drown out the crying baby in the motel room next to his. He looked over at the computer with his eyes squinted, realizing he was falling asleep while daydreaming about Eliza washing his car after changing the oil and completing a full tune-up.

"Hmm?" was the only sound he got out while reaching for the computer. Opening the lid, he had to blink several times to get his eyes to focus. Finally finding what had changed on the screen, he clicked on the red-circled number one over the notification icon.

E's Auto Body and Repair agreed with your comment. 5m ago.

He blinked one more time before reading the notification again. He clicked on it, waiting impatiently for the video sharing site to take him to the comment he posted. When the screen finished updating, his eyes locked onto the text with his username next to it.

You have a nice Supra.

"Holy shit." Gripping the laptop tight, he hopped off of the couch and screamed those words a second time. "Holy shit!" His eyes now wide, he checked again and saw the indicator icon lit that E's Auto Body and Repair approved of his comment.

"Holy shit. Holy shit!"

Muffled through the walls of the neighboring room with the screaming baby, he could faintly hear, "Hey, quiet down, my baby is sleeping!"

"Fuck off," he yelled. "She knows I exist."

He dropped back down onto the seat behind him. "She knows I exist." He read his comment again and stared at the icon next to it lit up by Eliza's interaction. His mind raced, wondering what he should do next. He opened another video posted by Eliza, clicked in the text box and began typing. The message he left behind looked like a child blabbering over a schoolyard crush. He slammed the laptop lid shut. "No, I need to do something more. Something that'll get her to focus on me and just me. Not these other people who are just hiding behind a keyboard."

Reaching into his pocket to retrieve his phone, he opened up the messages and found one near the top with a short exchange. Typing in the small box, he was less concerned about his spelling and grammar to this individual.

I want to do it.

Before he could set the phone down, it lit up with a new message. He was surprised, but excited to have an immediate response.

Great! I'm ready. When?

"Now," he said to himself, knowing that that wasn't possible and that he'd have to make an additional stop beforehand. He put some thought behind his response, making sure that he wouldn't have to change his answer and risk his best opportunity yet to make a lasting impression on Eliza.

I just need two days.

After sending the message, he stared at the lit screen for what felt like an eternity. He began to worry that the person on the other side wouldn't like the answer. That it was too long of a period of time. Maybe they would move on. Choose someone else. Lying to himself, he opened the box to begin typing another message.

Tomorrow. I can do tomor—

A new message came in, displayed above his partially typed fib.

Two days is perfect. I will see you then.

He held the backspace key on the phone's keyboard, clearing out the text before risking sending it.

"Two days," he said to himself. Using his phone, he quickly searched for the closest location of his bank. Finding one within a ten-mile radius, his excitement increased. "I'll get the money and get over there in two days. After that, a personal appointment with Eliza."

CHAPTER 17 - His New Found Confidence

"Hey, E?"

"Yeah, Allie? What's up?" Eliza asked from under the hood of a Miata.

"Don't you have to leave in a little bit to pick up your niece?" Allie responded.

"I have to get this air filter in and then I'll be done. What time is it anyway?"

"It's almost 11:30."

"That's plenty of time." Eliza snapped the last latch in place, carefully angled her head to not hit it on the open hood, and stood and stretched.

Allie looked at her boss's oil-covered hands and coveralls. "Is it though?"

Noticing that Allie wasn't looking at her eyes, and instead down at her chest, she followed the gaze to a large oil stain. With a poorly done Old English accent, she said, "I 'ad a gusher on this one. It just wouldn't stop bleedin'." She wiped her palms across the front of the coveralls and headed to the shop sink. Grabbing the pumice stone, she began rubbing her hands vigorously, watching the dingy water flow down the drain.

"Girl, you're going to tear your hands up. Shouldn't you be wearing gloves while doing that work?"

Hands dripping with water, Eliza pointed to a pile of broken rubber gloves near the front bumper of the Miata. "I tried. They kept getting caught while I was trying to get that last clip in place." After rubbing at one stubborn stain on her thumb, she dried off her hands on the shop towel, then unbuttoned the clasps on her coveralls. Allowing the top half to drop, she addressed Allie, "You're sure you're fine closing up tonight? I can come back with Nilah if you need me to."

"E, I know what I'm doing here. I'll keep my hands off the cars, ring up any customers that come in, and lock up everything when I'm done."

"And keep your hands off the customers," Eliza playfully added.

"If I must."

"You must. So, only if you're sure you don't mind?" Eliza had no reason to think that Allie wouldn't be able to handle the task, but had never requested her do it all herself in the almost decade she worked with her. "I'll get the garage bay doors when I walk out." Thinking through the other possibilities, she continued, "No one should be picking up cars today. And it's rare for anyone to drop off on a Friday afternoon, knowing that they won't see their car again until Monday."

"I know, E."

"And if anyone is crazy enough, just take down their details. You can drop me a message and I can send you a time estimate back."

"I'm not going to do that."

The two women glared at each other for a moment before simultaneously breaking their line of sight and laughing.

"Just go have fun with your niece, E. Take a break."

"I'm not sure it'll be a break, but it will be good to spend the weekend with her." She thought back to the last time she was alone with Nilah. Eliza had taken her niece to a park for a two-hour babysitting session while Johnny and Lindsay went to dinner for their anniversary. Prior, Eliza had spent the night at her brother's house after not feeling comfortable driving home when the wine was free-flowing. She awoke in the morning to find Nilah in the guest room bed with her. Her niece's tiny body was pressed against her back. But Eliza had never had Nilah for an entire weekend, and not at her own place.

"Good luck, and godspeed," Allie interrupted her thoughts. "Now get out of here or you'll be late."

"I still have plenty of time." Sliding the coveralls off the rest of the way, Eliza revealed a tight-fitting band T-shirt and denim shorts. She replaced her steel toe boots with a pair of running shoes she had left near the entrance of the garage, knowing she might be chasing her niece around almost immediately. Ushering Allie into the shop lobby, she looked back into the garage before reaching for the light switch. She stopped upon noticing the broken rubber gloves on the ground. She walked back to the Miata, patting it on the side fender before reaching down to snatch the gloves between two fingers, trying not to dirty her hands again. Once she was happy with the state of the shop, she met Allie in the lobby. "Thanks, Al. Let me know if you need me for anything."

"Go," Allie insisted.

After sticking her tongue out, Eliza turned and walked out the door. Making a quick check of the garage bay doors and verifying they were locked from the outside, she got in her car and headed toward her brother's house.

He finished the rest of his lunch, and felt a new surge of confidence after his recent purchase. After cleaning up, he drove directly to E's Auto Body and Repair.

Once pulled into the lot, he was surprised when he didn't see the white and red Supra parked in its normal spot. He figured it must be behind one of the garage bay doors. "She's always here. She must be working on her own car." He thought back to two nights ago; the online interaction that he had had with Eliza on the video of her car. His praise of it and her approval back.

Being in the actual lot of E's Auto Body and Repair, and not parked across the street, felt like euphoria to him. This part was easier than he expected. But psyching himself up to leave the car and go into the building was another feat. His imagination took over.

Upon entering the lobby of the auto shop, Eliza greeted him with outstretched arms.

"So you're the one who likes my car!"

He grinned. "It's the best car I've ever seen."

"Thank you so much. I'll do whatever you need me to do to yours. We can make them match. How wonderful would that be?"

He reached his arms out to return the embracing welcome.

Backfiring exhaust from a racing car on the street brought him back to reality. The front door of the shop with the flashing *Open* sign called to him, luring him from his safety inside the vehicle, like a fish to a worm on a hook. He felt like a bystander to his own body, watching himself walk to the door. His heart pounded, trying to escape from his chest with each beat.

The heat from the afternoon sun warmed the door handle of the building to a blissful temperature. After grabbing it, and holding it for an unnecessarily long time, he finally opened the door. The bell chimed above and broke his trance.

"You're back already?" a woman's voice said from behind the counter.

That's not the right voice, he thought. He'd watched each of Eliza's videos more than once. He'd been in the brewpub hearing her talk. He knew what she sounded like. Maybe it was muffled.

"I'm—" he began as the source of the voice stood and addressed him.

"Oh, hi! Sorry!"

The woman behind the counter had short hair with colored streaks down the right side. A small diamond piercing in her nostril sparkled from the lobby lights as she tilted her head slightly back and forth.

Where was Eliza? This wasn't her. Did he go to the right place? Her car wasn't outside. She wasn't standing in front of him now. He looked at the wall behind the counter, noting the logo of a tire with surrounding text that stared back at him. *E's Auto Body and Repair,* it said. No, this was the right place. So where was Eliza?

"I thought you were someone else. How can I help you?" the woman asked him.

"I, uh." At a loss for words, he tried to find something intelligent to say. "I wanted to—" He looked around. Where was Eliza? If she was there, he'd know what to say. He hoped he knew what he would say, anyway. His eyes landed on the lobby's merchandise. "I, uh. I need one of these." He reached for a circular gauge hanging from a hook on the wall. Pulling it down, and ignoring the price tag on it, he stuck it on the counter.

"Great," the bubbly voice said. "Anything else?"

"N—no," he lied. He wanted to talk to Eliza. He looked toward the door to the garage bays. It was dark inside. Was she not in there? Maybe the window was tinted. That would make sense, he realized.

"$77.16," the woman requested.

Reaching in his back pocket, he removed his wallet and thumbed through his cash. Luckily, there was more than enough for the unexpected expense. Pulling out two fifty-dollar bills, he handed them to the person behind the counter. His courage slowly rebuilt after seeing the sign for E's Auto Body and Repair directly over the head of the short-haired woman. He pointed toward the sign. "Is—" Fighting with the words, he slowly strung them together. "Is she—"

While counting out his change, the employee turned her head to see where he was pointing. "Are you looking for Eliza?" she asked him.

Only getting a nod out, he waited anxiously for her response.

"Sorry, dear. She stepped out for the day. She'll be back on Monday."

The woman suddenly leaned toward him. He almost jumped before noticing her hand held out a few bills and coins. As he reached for the money, she laid her other hand over the top of his.

"But *I* can help you if you need." Both of the woman's eyes opened wide. The sparkle of the nose ring brightened as she moved closer.

"N—no. I'll come back. Monday?" He pulled his hand away, dropping several coins on the counter. The unexpected interaction left him disoriented. Another plan to talk to Eliza had failed. He turned to leave.

"You forgot your gauge," the woman said. "And your change."

He swung back, grabbed the gauge, and sprinted toward the door. "Keep. Change," was all he could get out.

Briskly approaching the car, he fumbled with the keys, not finding the correct one to unlock the vehicle. He was pulling on the handle of the locked car with his other hand before he finally heard the click that allowed him back into the safety of his sheet metal cocoon.

His spontaneous purchase was thrown onto the pristine floor of the back seat. Unhappy with how poorly the last ten minutes had gone, he slammed his hands on the steering wheel. *Where is Eliza? Why isn't she here?* He moved his frustration to the roof of the vehicle, punching the gray headliner several times. *Dammit!* He composed himself, then started the car and began a distracted drive to his motel.

CHAPTER 18 - Nilah

"Aunt 'liza's here!" Nilah shouted when she heard knocking at the front door.

"Nilah!" Lindsay shouted as her daughter ran past her. "Get your toys off the floor before Aunt Eliza trips on them, please."

Grabbing one of the five different-sized stuffed animals in the hallway, and ignoring the dump truck that it was sitting in, Nilah answered, "Okay, Mommy." She continued to the window beside the front door and looked out the curtain. "Mommy, can I—"

"Yes, you can open it," Lindsay said, crouching over to pick up the remaining toys that Nilah left behind.

"Aunt 'liza!" the young girl exclaimed at the sight of her aunt standing on the porch. Pushing the screen door open, Nilah yelled toward the driveway, "Hi, Daddy. Whatcha doing?" She stepped past her aunt, holding the door just long enough for Eliza to step in and find Lindsay with her arms full of fluffy animals.

Before Eliza could greet her sister-in-law, Nilah ran back into the house. The screen door slammed shut behind her. Wrapping her arms around her aunt's legs, Nilah said, "I'm ready to go with you. Let's go."

"Ni, not yet. You need to get your books, toothbrush, and stuffie," her mom announced. "Hey, Eliza," she added calmly.

Chuckling slightly at the chaos, Eliza finally addressed Lindsay, "Hey. Need help with that stuff?" She hoped the answer would be no because she didn't know where anything would go, but reached out her arms, regardless.

"Nah. I got it." Lindsay quickly spun around. "Nilah! Where did you go?"

Relieved at Lindsay's response, Eliza questioned what her brother was doing outside. "Please tell me Johnny's not out there cleaning the car for me."

The sound of the shop vac outside starting caused Lindsay to speak up. "You know him. There's no way he would let you borrow a dirty car."

"Was it really *that* dirty?" Eliza questioned.

The eye roll Lindsay delivered told Eliza that the car was already plenty clean. It was a habit that both her and Johnny had learned from growing up with a father who took care of his vehicles with the same love that he showed his own two children.

"Got it," Eliza replied. Stepping further into the large single-family house and around the staircase, Eliza stopped to look at a picture on the wall of Johnny, Lindsay, and a newborn Nilah. Immediately next to the frame was another taken on the same day. It showed Eliza holding Nilah. The radiant smile on Eliza's face in the picture always reappeared any time she was around her niece.

"Your hair has gotten a lot longer since that picture was taken," Lindsay said while squeezing behind Eliza in the narrow hall, her hands still full of Nilah's toys.

"I'd cut it back off, but—" Eliza stopped herself, reaching for her right eye to find the bruise no longer hurt. "Maybe one day."

The front door slammed again, causing Eliza to jump. She turned her focus to the shadow approaching her.

"When did you get here, Li?" Johnny asked. "I saw your car parked out front."

She muttered obscenities in her head from the scare her brother gave her, but replied out loud with, "A few minutes ago. Not long. Why ya cleaning the car?" She tilted her head in the direction of Johnny's vehicle parked outside.

He simply shrugged. "It was dirty."

"Don't you have to leave soon? I promise I won't care if there's some dirt in the car."

"Less dirt. More cereal. All in Nilah's car seat." Realizing what he just said, he turned to face his sister. "Do you know how to put Ni in her car seat?"

"Shit. No." Catching her use of profanity, Eliza looked around to see if Nilah was in earshot.

"Good. She knows how to do it herself, anyway." The wink from Johnny made Eliza scrunch up her face at him.

"Jerk."

"That's not niiiiice," a young voice came from behind.

"What else did you hear?" Johnny replied with a wry grin.

"Nothing. I was in the bathroom."

Lindsay seemingly used her sixth sense when calling to her daughter on the other side of the house, "Nilah! Did you wash your hands?"

The march of Nilah back to the bathroom relieved the tension built up in Eliza from her use of questionable language and her brother picking on her as he always did.

Finally making her way into the living room, Eliza was surprised to see none of the three members of the household were ready to leave. She watched Johnny head to the kitchen sink wearing a ratty T-shirt with shorts ripped at the bottom seam. He picked up the same type of pumice soap she used for cleaning oil off of her hands to do the same for his grime-covered skin. In the adjacent room, Lindsay was picking up more toys, asking Johnny to bring the suitcase down from their bedroom when he was done. Nilah walked into the room wearing only one sock. Her wet, swinging hands caused small droplets of water to hit the back of Eliza's bare legs.

The grin in the picture Eliza had seen prior to entering the room suddenly appeared on her face. "Come here, you." Crouching down, she wrapped her arms around Nilah and gave her a light squeeze. "Do you know that you're my favorite?"

"I am?" the little girl asked with pure intrigue.

"You are. Now let's see if we can help your mom and dad, so we can get you to my home faster."

"Okay!"

Eliza traded a single key fob with a tiny race car keychain for her brother's stack of house keys, work machinery keys, and the key fob to his CR-V. She glared at Johnny while dangling the nearly two-pound stack in front of her.

"No," Eliza said flatly.

"No?" he asked.

"I'm not carrying all of this."

He reached out his hand, motioning for her to give back the jingling rat's nest. Once she obliged, he plucked the key fob for his SUV off of its valet key and handed the small rectangular device to Eliza.

"Better?"

"Much," she replied.

"Nilah," Johnny called across the room. "It's time for you to go with Aunt Eliza."

The squeak of the girl's still bare foot rubbing across the hardwood floor alerted the adults that she was on her way.

"Ni," Lindsay started, one hand resting on the suitcase near the front door, "Where's your other sock?"

Hopping on her bare foot, Nilah pulled a sock off her covered foot, revealing another sock underneath, and held it up for her mother to see. "Right here." She plopped down on the floor in between the grownups and put the newfound piece of apparel on. Once done, she made sure to show everyone that both feet were ready.

Lindsay ran through the mental checklist of things that Nilah would need while away from home for a few days, and looked at the three oversized bags used to house those items. She made another request for her daughter. "Get shoes, and then come give me a hug."

After giving her mother a hug, Nilah proceeded to wrap her arms around Johnny, and then ran off to the back of the house.

Eliza was the first to speak out. "Nilah, the car is out front."

"But my shoes are back here." Returning to the front entrance, carrying glitter-covered sneakers and sitting in the same spot as earlier, she finally followed Lindsay's first request. "Ready!" Nilah announced. She then opened the front door and walked outside.

Taking the cue from her niece, Eliza addressed Johnny and Lindsay. "Enjoy your trip." She slung two of Nilah's bags over her shoulder and picked up the third. She finished with, "See you in a few days. Be careful."

"Li, if you have any problems, don't hesitate to call," Johnny said. "Phone reception out there is usually decent."

Lindsay remained quiet but pleaded with her eyes for her sister-in-law to keep Nilah safe.

"We'll have fun," Eliza said. Thinking about the different kid-based activities that she had looked up in the surrounding area, she added, "I haven't been to the zoo in ages."

Eliza walked through the doorway, leaving Nilah's parents behind, and found the young girl already sitting in her car seat in the CR-V. When she realized that her brother had left his car unlocked, she took a quick glance at her Supra at the bottom of the driveway and hoped he wouldn't do the same with hers. She would send him a message later to make sure.

Eliza called into the vehicle to her niece, "You ready, kiddo?"

"Yeah!" Nilah replied enthusiastically.

"Then let's go."

CHAPTER 19 - His Job

We had a deadline today. Where have you been? Jayce keeps asking why you haven't been at work and I've run out of excuses to make for you. I thought you were only going to be out through Monday, and now you haven't been back at all this week either. For your sake, you better hope you're really sick or your fourth—or is it fifth now?—grandmother died.

"Fuck off," he said while clearing out his work email from his personal laptop. "If only they knew how close I was to Eliza, they'd understand why I haven't been back." He finished reading the rest of the message.

PS: I hope your grandmother is okay.

PPS: Start clearing out your browser history, dude. IT was asked to check it to see if they could figure out why you weren't here, and your entire history is nothing but these car tutorial videos. That shop isn't even around here. She is kind of cute, though. I started watching a couple, so I guess I get it. But really, just read the news like the rest of us do when we have down time.

He had the mouse cursor over the trash can icon next to the message, ready to send it into the nether, until he read the last part.

"He better not . . . That . . . I'm going to . . ." He began furiously typing a reply.

Stay off of my computer, asshole. And don't be watching those videos. Those videos are for me. She's talking to me, and no one else. When I get back there, if I find you watching one, I'm gonna roll you and your chair right out the window and drop your computer on top of your head.

He hit the *Send* button for the message, then selected the rest of the unread items in his inbox. No longer caring what anyone else had to tell him, he smashed the delete key on the keyboard. He began to lower the lid on the laptop until a sound alerted him that another new email had come in.

He had prepared himself to delete it immediately, seeing that it was a reply from his coworker, but enough of the preview caught his attention.

Your attitude is why no one likes you. Jumping down people's throats, obsessing over random shit. I probably wouldn't talk to you either if you didn't li—

"Fuck you," he said out loud again. He clicked the trash can icon next to the message and shut the lid. "Fire me, for all I care."

His annoyance at the messages made him search the room for something to take his mind away from work. He looked at the dirty motel room carpet, trying to will himself to run through his strength training routine; a regimen that he usually performed on the third and fourth watch-throughs of Eliza's videos. The work email put him off from using his laptop for the next couple of hours. He knew he still had to shower, so any sweat he'd work up, and grime from the room, would be removed as soon as he could. His phone would suffice for listening to Eliza's voice. Hearing it encouraged him to maintain his physique and keep his body as polished as any automotive body she would dare touch.

He loaded a video that he had only played through twice and began his routine. He tried to keep his head as close to the phone as possible, when the particular exercise allowed. Twenty pushups. Ten squats. Thirty-second plank. Fifteen crunches. Twenty lunges. Not having a pull-up bar in the motel room meant he had to skip the chin-up and pull-up reps. He continued the routine until the video stopped.

That must have been a shorter video, he thought. He wasn't sweating or straining at the end as much as he had expected. The carpet under him was still dry, showing no evidence of a recent salty rain shower. Any stains he saw were already there. He thought about starting another video and continuing on, but decided that for the next one he wanted to see Eliza, not just hear her.

He pulled off his shirt, marked with small sweat stains around his armpits and chest and threw it into the corner of the room. Rummaging through his set of belongings, he found a full plastic resealable bag and dumped out its contents. In his free hand, he held out his phone and started scrolling up. After he stopped, he tapped the image at the top of the screen and then turned the volume up until it maxed out.

With the resealable bag open, he placed the phone inside and closed the bag tight. From inside the thin plastic casing, a slightly muffled voice came through.

"Um, hi." The voice had an underlying nervousness to it. "I'm Eliza and I'm the shop. I mean, my shop is E's Auto Body and Repair. I want to show you a video on how you can check your car tire's air pressure."

He took the phone and its protective housing with him to the bathroom. A sink, toilet, and freestanding shower greeted him. The nicotine coated walls were covered in yellowish brown dried tears, a result of the high humidity of the shower mixing with the residue. A bleached white bath towel hung on a rack for him. After reaching in the shower to start the water, he stripped off the rest of his sweat-marked clothes. Grasping the bag with the phone in it, he took the decade-younger digital memory of Eliza with him into the warm water.

CHAPTER 20 - Nilah's Weekend

"What do you want to do first today?" Eliza asked a messy-haired Nilah. Her niece was sitting on the sofa in the apartment with a book in her lap. The morning sun provided enough light for the young girl to see the pages as she flipped through them.

Not immediately looking up, Nilah answered, "Pancakes." Upon realizing she wasn't in her own home, and that it was her aunt who asked her the question, she popped out of the chair and rushed to give Eliza a hug.

After bracing for the collision, Eliza gripped the young girl back. With Nilah in her arms, she thought about which options to suggest for the day's activities. The morning would be cooler than the afternoon, so Eliza offered several choices in a specific order. "How about we go to the zoo this morning, and then we can go to the mall? After that, maybe swimming in the pool here?"

"Will there be piggies at the zoo? Can I take my piggy stuffie, so it can see the piggies too? What's at the mall? Do I need money? I don't have any money. Do you have any money? Yay, pool! Let's go!"

Running through the various thoughts that went through her head while Nilah was spouting off what seemed to be a thousand questions, Eliza decided that pancakes actually sounded like a good idea for breakfast. The only problem, she realized, was that she didn't have pancake mix. When she remembered that she had flour, a recent purchase from when she decided she was going to bake bread when she found free time, she looked up the rest of the ingredients needed.

"Nilah, hold on just one second and I'll answer all of your questions. Okay?"

The young girl, whose face was already back in her book, simply replied with a nod.

After finding a recipe needing minimal ingredients, Eliza ticked off each item in her mental checklist, knowing she had also bought milk on the same shopping trip as the flour since Nilah would be over. She paused when finding out baking powder was needed. A substitution list for the ingredient she was sure she didn't have was shown, causing her to follow the link on the web page to the options. Eliza sighed with relief when she read that baking soda and cream of tartar could be used as a replacement. The natural polishing uses of each was one of the primary reasons for having each ingredient on hand. She wouldn't have the cream of tartar otherwise. Once she was sure she had all of the necessities to make their breakfast, Eliza finally spoke to Nilah again.

"Can you help me make the pancakes?"

Nilah's head spun around to meet her aunt's eyes. "Pancakes?" she asked.

"Yup. Would you like to help?"

Nilah tossed her book, popped up from the couch, then ran into the kitchen. "Don't we need a bowl, Aunt 'liza? And a spoon? I can't reach the counter. Do you have a chair I can stand on?"

Eliza grinned at the barrage of new questions.

"I can't eat any more," Nilah said as she played with the dollop of syrup that she dropped on the table while eating her pancakes.

"Me neither," Eliza responded. Watching the child's finger get stuck to the table and then pulled back up over and over, she offered her niece praise for her work. "You made really yummy pancakes. Thanks for your help."

Nilah nodded her head in agreement and then stuck the syrup-covered finger in her mouth. "Mmm," she mumbled.

Eliza stared at the stuffed pig in the chair next to Nilah at the small kitchen table. Remembering one of the many questions the girl had fired off before they ate their breakfast, Eliza asked, "Does the zoo still sound good this morning? And yes, piggy can come."

The finger in Nilah's mouth popped out, and the hand attached to it reached for the stuffed animal. "Did you hear that, piggy? We're going to the zoo!"

Eliza grabbed the plates and utensils from the table to place in the kitchen sink before realizing what else needed to be done before leaving the apartment with her niece. "Nilah, can you go wash your hands? And do you know where your clothes are?" Wondering how long it would take to get the girl dressed, she also thought about what she should do with Nilah's hair, hoping that Lindsay packed a brush. She didn't remember seeing one when pulling out the girl's toothbrush the night before, but maybe it was in another bag. After looking at the clock, Eliza was surprised to see that it was still early, so they might make it to the zoo before it got too crowded. When she heard the water running in the bathroom, Eliza was pleased that one of the things that needed to be done was already being accomplished.

The sights and smells of the local zoo overwhelmed Eliza's senses as she looked around at the signs directing her and her niece to the different animal enclosures. She held Nilah's hand while navigating through the small crowd of people as they entered the attraction when it opened. Eliza couldn't remember the last time she was at this zoo, and nothing about it looked familiar. As a child on a school field trip, she would have followed her teacher or a parent chaperone through the zigzagging pathways, but she had never navigated it herself.

"Can we play hide and seek?" Nilah suddenly asked. The young girl appeared excited about the possibilities the large area provided. "This looks like a great place for hide and seek. I love hide and seek."

The question caused Eliza to tighten her grip on Nilah's hand. "No," flew out of her mouth without having an explanation available. Nilah's look of disappointment made her give the girl a reason. "This is not a good place for it. I would never be able to find you and I would be really sad. Maybe when we get back to my apartment. Somewhere much smaller and with less people, okay?"

"Okay." The answer seemed to satisfy the young girl. "What animals will we go see first?" In her free hand, Nilah held up the stuffed pig she brought with her, indicating that the question was intended for the toy and not for her aunt.

Eliza looked at the paper map she grabbed near the entrance when they walked in. She traced the paths with her eyes. After finding the location she was looking for, she addressed Nilah, "The domestic animals are over—"

"What are do-mes-tic animals?" Nilah immediately interrupted.

"Horses, and chickens, and—" she paused and crouched down to Nilah's level, knowing how excited the girl would be for the last one. "Pigs! Farm animals. Those are domestic animals."

"Oh, piggies! Where are they?" Nilah's head swiveled, trying to find where the animals would be.

"We'll have to walk to them. But right now, we're near the rhinoceroses and the giraffes. Then we'll make it past the monkeys and zebras. Then you two—" Eliza looked back and forth between her niece and the stuffed animal "—can see the pigs."

The feeling of wandering the zoo like a child made Eliza appreciate the opportunity to spend the weekend with Nilah. It had been so long since she had taken time to herself, not focusing on her shop, or creating the online content for it, that she had forgotten about the other activities that she enjoyed. Half-watching the zebra move around in the animal enclosure in front of them, Eliza looked down at the wide-eyed young girl pushed up against her. Eliza wrapped her arm around Nilah, pulling her in tight, and felt the girl snuggle in. The feeling of pure love that rushed through Eliza made her involuntarily squeeze Nilah even tighter. Snapping back to the purpose of their trip, Eliza asked the question that she already knew the answer to. "Ready to find the pigs?"

"Yeah!" Nilah started walking, heading in the direction they had come from.

"Ni, don't walk off without me, please. And we have to go this way, unless you want to see the lions again."

"No lions. Piggies." She turned around and rejoined her aunt, waiting for Eliza to guide them to the snorting animal.

During the walk to the farm animals, Eliza was happy to see there were less people around, and released her grip on her niece's hand, letting Nilah walk a short distance ahead of her. Eliza's stomach growled like a clock chiming that it was nearly noon, answering the unasked question of where everyone had gone.

"Nilah, how about we head to the mall after we see the pigs? We can get some lunch there. Maybe hamburgers with fresh bacon." The easy joke about the source of the bacon fell flat with her niece, but Eliza was happy when no additional questions were asked.

"I can see the horses, but where are the piggies? Piggy, piggy, where are you?" Nilah walked around the enclosure, becoming visibly disappointed that she was unable to find the animal she was most excited to see.

"Ni, here, look." Eliza stopped a few paces behind Nilah and glanced toward an opening of a small wooden shack. The short-legged, stout-bodied animal sauntered out when Nilah passed. "Here comes Mr. Pig now."

Nilah spun on her heels and rushed back to Eliza. "Ewww," she announced when she saw it.

"Ew?" Eliza questioned, genuinely surprised at the girl's reaction.

"Yeah. Ew. It's not all fluffy like my stuffie." Holding up the stuffed pig, and comparing it to the two-hundred pound animal walking to the mud pit, Nilah again said, "Ew."

Eliza stifled a laugh, unsure of what to say at first. "Nilah. This is what a real pig looks like." She crouched down next to her niece. "Oh! Nilah, look!" Eliza saw a piglet walk out of the wood structure, knowing that Nilah would be more interested in the baby animal.

"Piggy! See, piggy?" Nilah turned the toy around so its eyes would face the live animals and spoke to it. "A piggy like you. This is the best day ever, Aunt 'liza."

The edges of Eliza's mouth ran out of space as the grin formed. Her heart melted at the joy the young girl was experiencing. "Let me take a picture to send to your mom and dad, okay? Turn around, and smile." Eliza pulled her phone out of her pocket and framed the picture to include the young girl holding the stuffed animal and the piglet. "Perfect. Now, ready to go eat?"

Nilah turned toward the piglet one last time. "Bye, piggy. It was nice to meet you."

CHAPTER 21 - His Weekend

The weekends had become the worst part of staying in the small town away from his home for the past few weeks. Eliza's shop was closed on Saturdays and Sundays, so he couldn't even park in the lot across from it to look over every detail of her Supra, hoping to get a glimpse of its owner.

The chance encounter in the elevator seemed to be a fluke. He never saw Eliza again in the apartment building where he first met her in person. After spending the first full week away from it, afraid he was going to get in trouble for what he did to Eliza, the draw of her pulled him back. When no punishment seemed imminent, he waited each weekend day in one of the apartment lobby chairs in hopes to find her. He wished to bump into her another time. Albeit with less force.

His friend who lived in the apartment complex started questioning seeing him there on multiple days, causing him to give up looking for Eliza in the building. He was running out of excuses and didn't think his acquaintance would buy the latest— that his car was being worked on at a nearby shop and he simply needed somewhere to sit. The friend suggested using the much more comfortable sofa in his apartment as a waiting area, pointing out that there was a TV available to watch to pass the time, but he refused the offer.

He spent several afternoons driving up and down the apartment building's parking garage looking for Eliza's car. The speed bumps were jarring and he memorized which turns he could take tight and which needed to be taken wide. After the second time he came head on with another vehicle, leaving horns blaring from both drivers, he gave up. He ultimately came to the dreadful conclusion that

Eliza did not live in that apartment building and was indeed visiting a friend, as he was, on that fateful day.

He couldn't return to her shop. He wanted to be direct with her, but the meeting needed to appear unintentional. The small shop was too intimate. It would leave him exposed.

He hadn't been able to bring himself to follow her home directly. He was the smartest person he knew, but he couldn't come up with a reason that would convince her to open her door for him. He wasn't some simple-minded delivery driver. He couldn't begin his life with her on a lie. No, he would rather she invite him to her sanctuary. Following her from her shop when she went out for lunch or to the brewpub was different in his mind, but once she reached residential areas he backed off. Accidentally finding her in an apartment was different than risking tracking her to a single-family home. He wanted to build up a friendship first, proving to her that they had plenty in common. Then he would show her that he could keep up with her in conversation, particularly about different automotive topics.

Sitting in his car outside of the motel, he had an epiphany. He had learned about tuning cars, and even doing some body work by watching Eliza's videos. He felt like he could speak intelligently about the different subjects, being able to recite each of the transcripts of her work verbatim, but he didn't have personal experience with another automotive pastime: street racing.

Here he was in an area with straight, flat roads. Something that wasn't available in the densely packed city where he lived. Eliza talked of speed. She talked of increasing horsepower. She talked about spending time at the track, and the excitement of watching cars compete to see which one would come out on top. He wanted to experience it himself.

He eased his car onto the street. Ahead, he saw a stoplight that was turning red on the straight two-lane road. Noticing another car coming up directly behind him, he moved to the empty lane and began to slow, allowing the other vehicle to catch up. The deep-throated exhaust pop from the second vehicle as it downshifted made him hopeful that he had already found a partner for his new lesson. The two cars stopped side-by-side at the red light. He dropped his car into neutral and pressed down the accelerator, causing the tachometer's needle to dip into the red. The quiet muffler still let out enough noise to get the attention of the driver next to him.

Looking over to the vehicle, he saw its owner turn their head toward him. A brief nod from the other driver, and a rev of the engine in response to the wordless question posed, made his heart race. He wasn't expecting to find a willing participant in this learning experience so quickly. With his attention now aimed at the traffic light in front of him, he shifted his car back into drive and held down the brake pedal, waiting for the signal to tell them to go. The thumping of his blood rushing through his body almost deafened him. He imagined it as gas coursing through the fuel lines in his car, ready to be ignited, providing the energy to move forward.

The light turned green. He moved his foot as quickly as he could from the brake to the accelerator, pushing the pedal down as far as it would go. A light thud sounded as it hit the floor. The chirp of his wheels was drowned out by the long screech of the tires of the vehicle next to him losing traction. He was ahead, a benefit of the rubber maintaining its grip after first coming off the line.

The buildings on the sides of the racing vehicles passed by at an exhilarating rate. The windows were no longer individual rectangles, but now appeared as one long, blurred jagged line. His heart rate steadied as his eyes stayed on the lines on the road.

The other car slowly inched ahead. Further up the road, he noticed another traffic light, still green in his direction. On the sides, cars were waiting for their turn to cross through the intersection. He hoped it wouldn't change before they got there. He wasn't ready to finish this first lesson. The other car was now a full car-length ahead. He looked around the inside of the cabin of his car, wondering if there was anything he could do. He wanted to go faster, didn't want to lose, and certainly didn't want to stop. He tapped the gear shifter to a lower gear. The tachometer's needle shot up again, like the second hand on a clock trying to escape. He was pushed back into his seat. It gave him enough of a boost to catch a few inches on his racing partner, but he still remained behind.

The traffic light was approaching fast, but had now turned yellow. He looked into the window of the other vehicle, noticing their attention was still forward. They didn't seem to be backing off, so that meant he wouldn't either.

The light turned red. They were still seventy-five yards away from it. Enough time to stop, but the other car wasn't slowing. He held his foot in place, moving the gear shifter back to a higher gear. The tachometer had been sitting in red for too long. He couldn't risk damaging the engine.

Cars crawled into the intersection. His racing partner squeezed through a gap before the two streams of cross-traffic vehicles were about to converge. He took the unspoken advice and moved his car behind the other, getting through before a silver SUV passed, barely missing his rear bumper.

"What in the actual fuck was that?" Eliza yelled. She was driving her brother's CR-V, niece in tow, to the mall from the zoo. The traffic light had turned green and she was nearing the middle of the intersection when two cars flew past. From a quick glance at the vehicles that went through the red light, she identified an Integra with a distinct scuff on the rear driver-side fender, prompting her to make a mental note to have a long chat with Oliver the next time she saw him.

The young girl in the backseat looked up from her book to ask her aunt, "Did you say something?"

Happy that they were both safe, and that her niece was lost in her story learning more age-appropriate words than the one she spat, Eliza thought about how to keep the girl's attention. She turned her head slightly to ask Nilah, "What was your *second* favorite animal at the zoo?"

"Hippos!"

"The hippos? Not the monkeys, or seals—" She decided to add one more option to get a rise from Nilah. "Or snakes?"

"No. Not the snakes. The hippos. They were fun to watch."

Eliza pictured the large animals standing in the water at the zoo, not doing much, and took the girl's word for what she considered fun. "Hippos it is. We're almost to the mall. Is there anything you want to eat?"

"Can I have French fries?"

"Of course you can have French fries, Ni. But think bigger. What else do you want?"

"Big French fries?" said Nilah, taking the phrase her aunt used literally.

"I was thinking something closer to ice cream, but I'm sure we can find big French fries too." Eliza smiled at the innocence of the young child, leaving her envious of Nilah's minimal wants and needs.

"Can I have both, please?"

After finding open parking near the entrance of the large building, Eliza pulled the vehicle into an empty spot, then answered Nilah's question. "Sure you can."

The adrenaline of the near collision a few minutes earlier had subsided, thanks to the distraction of the conversation with Nilah. Normally, a dangerous situation involving modified vehicles would have left her seething, knowing that people like that gave a bad rep to the kind of work she did. While her shop could handle the regular oil change, air filter replacement, and tire rotation, E's Auto Body and Repair was known for performance upgrades and visual modifications. She hated when she became associated with, and blamed for, the troublemakers. Knowing the owner of one of the problem cars made it worse, and she wouldn't let it go.

CHAPTER 22 - Finally on Vacation

"It's peaceful here, Johnny."

He barely caught the underlying tone in Lindsay's voice and asked matter-of-factly, "You miss Nilah's incessant questions this early in the morning, don't you?" A wink in the direction of his wife punctuated his question as he took a sip of his hot coffee, the steam from it fading into the cool morning air. The aroma from the beverage and the strong bitter flavor made him close his eyes to soak in the moment of quiet. It had been ages since he was able to enjoy a cup of coffee and not use it only to wake up enough to be functional for the day.

"Of course I do. I'm not used to it being *this* quiet, though. I'm not complaining. *Peaceful* is needed, no matter how out of the ordinary it has become." Following suit, Lindsay cupped her mug in both hands and blew across the top of it before taking a sip. She stared out at the lake as the pair sat in rocking chairs on the back porch of their rented cabin.

"What do you want to do today?" Johnny asked while checking the weather on his phone. The weak cell phone signal caused a delay in the data to come through. Finally seeing the icon of rain and thunder for the following day, the same day they would leave in the evening to get home to Nilah, he continued, "This might be our nicest day. I could sit and look at the lake all day, but if you want to hike the falls, or get out on the canoe, it might have to be today."

Taking another sip from her mug, Lindsay looked over at her husband. "So, we'll be stuck indoors all day tomorrow, huh? And all alone?"

The context of the comment was easily understood. Johnny turned his head toward Lindsay while trying to decide how best to respond. After a few choice thoughts ran through his head, he decided to use the one that was most likely to get a reaction from his wife. "I'm sure we could find some friends to invite over." Nodding to the cabin, he added, "Most of the board games in there need four players."

Lindsay expected a response very close to what she received, one that did not involve them spending time together in their bedroom. "I saw cards in there. You can practice your solitaire."

Admitting defeat, Johnny smirked, loving the uninterrupted, playful bickering with his wife, and took the final gulp of his coffee.

"The level is really high compared to the last time we were here," Johnny said to Lindsay, speaking loudly while watching the flow from the waterfall into the stream below. The breeze created from the rapid movement of the falling water and the spray kicked up into the air felt nice on his exposed skin. "When we drove over the bridge to get here, I thought it looked different, but wondered if it was the amount of time since our last trip playing tricks on me." Johnny looked at the erosion line along the river, barely visible from the height of the water. Recalling some recent news he came across, he wondered if the storms sitting over the counties further north were feeding the river. "Much more and it might actually cover the road."

The shining sun warmed the couple, causing Lindsay to remove her boots and step into a small offshoot of the river from a tiny pebble beach. Nervously watching his wife, Johnny held back his worry, knowing that she wouldn't venture further into the swift moving water. He knew that Lindsay was a strong swimmer from her college days, and a lifeguard as one of her first jobs, but it didn't fully tame his concern. He stayed back, not wanting to get his own feet wet, but watched Lindsay enjoy the refreshing wade.

"What are you looking at?" Lindsay questioned when noticing Johnny was staring at her.

In response, Johnny blew his wife a kiss and settled down on a large stone nearby. The sun's rays speckled him through the gaps between the leaves of the trees. "Just the view. I'm good to keep going whenever you are."

"You look comfortable," she said.

"My butt is already going numb. The rock is too hard." He squinted at her. "Can you help?"

Lindsay stuck her hand in the river, closed her fingers together to form a cup, and threw water at Johnny. "How's that?" Returning her hand to the river, she added, "Will another help?"

The cool water felt refreshing, but as Johnny wiped the drips off of his face while looking down at his splattered clothes, he replied, "No, no, one was enough." He stood when he saw Lindsay returning to dry land, readying herself to keep walking.

The sun shining through the glass of wine sitting in front of Lindsay left a long, red, glowing streak on the table. Lost in the blood-like image, she almost didn't notice when Johnny rejoined her with a new drink of his own.

"What are you thinking about?" he asked, moving the chair so his view from the winery overlooked the lake in the distance.

"You said it's supposed to rain tomorrow?" She picked up her glass and watched the caustic light appear to flow off the edge of the table.

"Yeah. It should start mid-morning."

"That sucks. I'm really enjoying this. I wouldn't mind getting back to the river." A sip of the wine passed through her lips and left a small tingling sensation as it went down her throat. "Mmm. And another glass of this."

"We'll see. The weather changes quickly." Johnny followed suit, taking a drink from his glass. "Maybe we'll luck out and get a chance to do a few more things before the rain." He looked behind him and through the large glass doors of the winery, seeing several tables inside. "We could still come back here and sit inside."

Holding out the glass in her hand, Lindsay replied, "This might not taste as good inside."

Johnny laughed. "Would that stop you from drinking it?"

Pressing the wine glass against her lips again, Lindsay tilted it so the remainder of the liquid entered her mouth. After holding it for a moment to appreciate the flavors, she swallowed and then replied, "No, but I'd be willing to take one for the team. But just in case, I better get another while I can still sit out here to enjoy it." She pushed her chair back and headed toward the winery doors. "Do you need anything?"

"Not yet." He twirled the liquid around in his glass. The higher sugar content of this particular varietal caused the wine legs to run slowly down. "This one is quite sweet. But it's not going to take me long to finish."

Without another word, Lindsay entered the building, leaving Johnny to take in the view by himself.

CHAPTER 23 - His New Skill

It was too dark under the shade of the vehicle's hood in the motel parking lot for him to see what he was reaching for in the back of the engine bay. He cursed as the socket wrench slipped from his gloved hands a second time, getting stuck rather than falling to the ground like the previous time he had dropped the tool.

He turned to the toolbox on the ground next to him. Curious about what else was in it, he began rummaging through the different sections, pulling out drawers and lifting the multiple tiers, looking for a pair of needle nose pliers, forceps, or at a minimum a flashlight. He gave up after finding nothing except a few basic screwdrivers and something that looked like it was used for gutting a fish. He wondered how the original owner of the toolbox ever got anything done with these tools. He looked back under the hood of the car and reached his arm deep inside.

"I can't get—" His fingers stretched. The side of the latex glove ripped as his hand dragged over the sharp edge of the clamp holding the air filter box closed. He pulled his hand out and removed the damaged glove, discarding it to the ground. After checking for dirt and grease on his hand and finding none, he grabbed a new glove from the pile sitting on the chassis. With a newly protected hand, he navigated the path to the socket wrench, avoiding the clamp. Stretching his fingers once again, he was able to brush the round metal handle.

He pushed his hand into the tight crevice and extended his digits as far as they would go. Finally able to wrap the tips of his pointer finger and middle finger around the tool, he pulled hard. He was initially pleased to see the socket wrench in his hand, but his heart skipped a beat after noticing a thin hose he hadn't seen before sticking up from the gap where his hand had exited.

While shifting his body around to the side of the engine compartment, he knocked over an empty plastic container that once contained the gauge he bought from E's Auto Body and Repair. Unconcerned with the litter, and scooting it aside with his foot, he reached for the jagged-ended black hose sticking out from behind the fuse box. He questioned himself on what he was holding. Not able to find where it should be connected, he gave up and got into the driver's seat. He removed the gloves he was wearing and tossed them out the car door. Gripping the steering wheel with both hands, he said a small prayer to the car gods before putting the key in the ignition and turning it.

The car started. He breathed a sigh of relief while staring up at the heavens, until the idle became erratic. The motion of the tachometer's bouncing needle caught his eye. He watched it drop to near zero before ricocheting back up and past its expected stopping point. A light on the dash took his attention away from the rhythmic movement.

He said the only word he could think of.

"Shit."

Looking at the newly-installed gauge on the dashboard showing a steady twelve volts from the car's battery, a quick smirk appeared on the corner of his mouth when he realized that, at a minimum, he hooked up the new device correctly. He had never done anything like this before. Watching Eliza's videos had given him a sliver of knowledge. Now, he felt he could show that he had the experience, not just regurgitate the information.

He returned to the front of the vehicle, regloved his hands, and grabbed the thin hose. He wasn't sure what to do about the damaged part. It was unlikely he could fix it himself. He knew of only two automotive shops in the area: E's Auto Body and Repair, and the shop that he stole the toolbox from after it was left unattended outside. He thought the five-finger discounted purchase full of automotive-specific tools would be ideal if he were to ever take his vehicle to Eliza's shop. He'd leave it in a location in his car for her to see. Immediately, he knew he wouldn't do that. He would be too embarrassed. How was he supposed to impress her if the first time he had to have a conversation about cars with her was to admit that he damaged his own and didn't know how to fix it?

Looking at the toolbox, he shut the hood of the car first, then closed the container housing the tools. He knew he couldn't keep it in the car when taking it to the other automotive shop, so he turned off the idling vehicle and carried the toolbox into his motel room.

The other shop was only two blocks down the road. He looked up the number and called it, praying again that it was open on a Sunday afternoon.

A voice on the other end of the line answered immediately. "This is Eric's Automotive. How can I help you?"

"Um." He hadn't had time to figure out what he needed to say, but was relieved that someone answered the phone. "I broke something."

"Okay, sir. On your car?"

The extra moment used up by the question gave him the opportunity to put together a cohesive thought. "Yes. On my car."

"And what did you break?" the man asked.

He heard the rustling sound of the phone being moved and a few keys on a keyboard being pressed.

"I installed a voltage gauge in my car, but as I was finishing up, I dropped a tool," he explained. "When retrieving it, I snagged a hose and must have pulled it out. I can't figure out where it needs to go and now the idle is rough."

"Oh, bummer, man. Sounds like a vacuum leak. The hose must have been part of the air filter line. If you want to bring the car by, I can take a look this afternoon. Um, it might take a little time, though, depending on when you get here." There was additional clacking of the keyboard before the man added, "Will you wait, or do you have a ride back?"

He knew the weather would allow him to return to the motel without a vehicle. He responded, "I can walk back. I'm not far."

"Sounds good. Bring 'er in when you can," said the voice on the other side of the phone call.

"Okay. Thanks."

"No, thank you."

After limping the car a few blocks to Eric's Automotive, he was happy that he didn't appear to do any more damage, and didn't need a tow. The voltage gauge he installed was working flawlessly, and the car still moved when pressing the accelerator pedal. The money involved to fix the car wasn't the issue, but his ego had already taken a hit when he was unable to fix the problem himself. He couldn't risk incompetence around Eliza.

Upon entering the shop and finding it empty, he waited awkwardly for a moment until a voice yelled from the open garage.

"I'm in here! Just give me a minute, boss. I'll be right there after I crawl out from underneath this car."

He looked around the dingy lobby, wishing he was standing in Eliza's shop. The walls there were clean. The floor was spotless. The selection of merchandise was large. And while not his type—she wasn't Eliza, after all—other customers likely didn't have complaints about the receptionist, even if she did come on a little strong. This shop had none of that.

The man in the garage came out to the small waiting area and introduced himself. "Hey, sorry to keep you waiting. I'm Eric. What can I do for you?" While waiting for a response, Eric used a rag to wipe off his greasy hands. The white T-shirt he was wearing looked as if it had already been used for the same.

"I, uh, called earlier." He would have preferred to be talking to Eliza. She was never this dirty. Not that he had seen. How did she do that? She worked on cars. Changed oil, too. Camera effects maybe? Wore gloves? Was much more careful? "The hose. The idle," he finally said to the man in front of him.

"Oh, yeah, right." Eric clapped his hands together. "Let me get the paperwork for you. I'll have you fill that out, grab your keys, and I'll get to it in . . . probably a couple hours? I just have this clutch I'm wrapping up."

A quick nod sent Eric on his way and left him alone. The thought of this man, professional mechanic or not, getting into his car with grease-covered clothing, made him cringe. But he knew he needed the vehicle in working order before he could bring it to Eliza to do some real upgrades. Things that would impress her. Not to have her fix his mistakes.

"Here you go, sir." Eric handed over a clipboard upon returning. "Just leave me a number to call. You said you can walk back, right? Don't need a ride? I have time, I could take you if you needed."

Looking around the shop, and noticing the lack of any other customers, he understood why Eric would be able to take him to the motel. He wouldn't want to anyway, but was sure he didn't want to see the state of the inside of Eric's own vehicle after seeing how the shop's lobby was kept. He tried to give him the benefit of the doubt. Seeing that there was no other help around, he guessed that Eric was probably busy working on cars most of the time and was less concerned about the outer appearances.

After writing the final piece of information on the paper in front of him, and wiping his hand on the side of his pants after placing down the greasy pen, he finally replied, "No, I'm fine. It's nice out and I, uh, could use the exercise."

"All right then. I'll call when I know more. Thanks again." Eric took the key for the car and returned to the garage, leaving him alone in the lobby.

Revulsion hit when he saw the new grease spot Eric left on the doorframe into the garage as the shop's owner used it for leverage to step down into the work area. Eager to get away from the grime, he started the walk back to his motel.

CHAPTER 24 - They're Late

Eliza saw her brother's name displayed on her phone and answered the call by the second ring.

"Hey, Johnny. What's up? Almost home?"

"Um, about that." The nervous tone in his voice came through the tiny speaker. "The rain hit earlier than expected. It's been pouring for hours and the bridge on the way out is underwater. They closed it."

Eliza could tell there was more coming, so she held back a response.

"If I had my CR-V, I could probably get across it."

Coming through the phone muffled, Eliza could hear Lindsay in the background correcting her husband. "That would have been dumb. You would have floated away and I would have stood on the side of the road and watched."

"Never mind," Johnny said. "Maybe I couldn't. Look, I'm sorry to have to do this, but you'll be okay with Nilah for another day, right? We could see if Lindsay's parents could drive up if not. The forecasters say this should clear by the end of the day, and the water should recede pretty quickly after. Once it does, we can head back. But it's not looking like it will be until tomorrow afternoon."

Without hesitation, Eliza responded, "Yeah, of course, John. Not a problem. Not like I could or would say no anyway." She quickly realized what her plan at the garage the next day entailed. "Hey, I'll have to take her to the shop, though. I have something I need to do for about an hour. Allie should be okay to watch her."

Johnny immediately replied, "Yeah, that's fine."

"What's fine?" Eliza heard Lindsay say in the background.

"Hold on, Li, I'm gonna put you on speaker." After a few clicks, Johnny continued talking, evident that he was addressing Lindsay. "She said she'd have to take Nilah to the shop with her, but Allie would be able to watch her there."

"That's fine. I trust Allie," Lindsay said.

"Me too," Eliza agreed. "Hey, do you guys want to talk to Nilah?" She knew the answer to the question before she finished asking and raised her voice to get the girl's attention while also switching to speakerphone on her end of the conversation. "Nilah, it's your mom and dad!"

"Mommy! Daddy!" Nilah called out.

"Hey, sweetie," Lindsay started the chat with her daughter. "Are you having fun with Aunt Eliza?"

"Yes."

"Would you like to stay with her for another day?"

"Yes!"

"That's good. Me and Daddy are stuck right now, so we're not going to be able to get home until tomorrow."

"But I want you home," Nilah said.

"I know, Nilah."

"Hey, Ni," Johnny jumped in to distract the girl. "What have you done with Aunt Eliza so far? How many new words has she taught you?"

Eliza bit her tongue at the implication of her teaching Nilah a few curse words, and allowed the young girl to answer.

"The zoo!" Nilah's mood quickly shifted. "We saw so many animals." Oinking like a pig, Nilah started running around the apartment.

"I'm glad you had fun."

"Nilah," Lindsay said. "Be good for another day, all right? We'll be home as soon as we can."

Nilah began honking and grunting like a hippopotamus in response.

"See you soon, Nilah. I love you," Johnny said.

"Love you, Ni," Lindsay repeated.

"I love you!" Nilah yelled back.

Eliza took the opportunity to ask her family about their trip. "Are you two at least having fun where you are? Are you stuck in your cabin, or can you at least get out and about?"

Johnny answered, "The rain is a little heavy right now. I don't know if you can hear it, but the size of these drops coming down is absurd. Once it subsides, there's a winery nearby that we'll probably go back to. The view will be a lot different than yester—"

"Very different," Lindsay huffed.

"But it'll help pass the time while we wait this out," Johnny finished.

"All right, well, be safe when you do get on the road," Eliza said. She would enjoy another day with Nilah, but wasn't sure what she would do if the stay extended much longer.

As if reading her mind, Johnny changed topics. "You still have the spare key to the house, right? If you need anything for Ni, you can swing by and get it."

"Yeah, I have it. Hopefully, I won't need it. We'll be fine. See you guys some time tomorrow?"

"Yup, thanks, Li. Bye."

After hanging up, Eliza turned to her niece and said, "It's just you and me for the rest of the day. What do you want to do?"

Nilah shrugged in response.

She considered the nearby motel with a playground next to it and the lake in view. "There's a park close by. It has a lake in the shape of a big horseshoe."

"No, thank you."

Eliza thought about the things she used to do with her dad as a kid, working on cars together being one of them. She wondered about having Nilah look over Johnny's CR-V with her, until remembering that she and her brother shared the same automotive obsessed parent. "I'd have you check out your dad's car with me, but I have a feeling it's in perfect working order. Isn't it?"

Nilah shrugged again.

"How about a movie?"

Nilah began nodding emphatically.

"Okay. A movie it is." She recalled part of her conversation with Johnny and Lindsay and said, "Tomorrow, I need to take you to my shop until your mom and dad get home, okay?"

"Yes," Nilah responded in a shy whisper.

"But we'll worry about that tomorrow. Let's pick out a movie to watch. What do you think? Talking cars?"

"Nope."

"What do you mean *nope?*" Eliza showed a silly side-eye. "Fine. Talking people?"

"But we're talking people."

"Then I guess you must want . . ." She let the seconds tick by for added effect. "Talking animals."

"Yeah! Talking piggies."

"I'm sure I can find a movie with talking piggies. Go get yourself comfortable while I look."

CHAPTER 25 - Grinded Beans

"Where's your car, Oli? Huh? Did you crash it? What the he—" Eliza looked down at her niece as they approached the front counter in the Grinded Beans coffee shop. She changed her word choice while she continued to berate her fellow small business owner. The empty cafe allowed her to do so without causing a scene in public. "What was with you blowing through that red light the other day? Were you racing that other car? I expected better from you." The pause she provided while trying to find the next way to scold Oliver without the use of her typical four-letter words gave him an opportunity to say something in his defense.

"I sold it."

"And another thi—" The gears in Eliza's mind ground to a halt. "What?"

"I sold it. I don't have the Integra anymore. I bought the Jeep that's out there. I can't afford a supercar," Oliver slipped in. "But the Jeep is new and seems to handle well." He gestured out the door at a black Jeep in the parking lot. Scanning the lot more extensively, a look of confusion on his face followed. "Where's the Supra?" he asked. He took the opportunity to pick on his friend and added, "Did you crash it?"

"Did I—" Eliza looked out the door. Seeing the silver CR-V parked where she normally parked her Supra, she replied, "Oh. No. I have my niece for the weekend. I'm borrowing my brother's car." Eliza patted the top of the girl's head. "Nilah, this is Mr. Oliver."

Nilah waved shyly.

Before returning to the adult conversation, Oliver asked Nilah, "Would you like a muffin?"

Nilah looked up at her aunt in a bid to ask for permission.

Eliza nodded. "You do. They're very yummy. I like the blueberry, but he also has chocolate."

Nilah turned her focus to Oliver and moved her head up and down rapidly.

"Chocolate?" Oliver asked.

The girl's head continued to move in the same direction.

Taking the cue, Oliver grabbed a chocolate muffin from the pastry case and handed it to Nilah before addressing Eliza. "I guess you saw the Integra recently?"

Once Oliver's comments about his car caught up to her, Eliza replied, "Yeah. I was driving Nilah to the mall from the zoo, and two cars, one being your Integra, flew through the intersection as I was starting to go through it. We got really lucky." She looked outside at the Jeep. "When did you sell it? You just had it in my shop."

"Not long ago. I think the day after I brought it in to you. I was there to have you give it a once over before I sold it, to make sure the buyer would be happy. I tried to tell you, but you were busy."

Eliza thought back to that day, remembering seeing Oliver in her shop after she returned from the police station. "Oh, right, sorry. I guess that's why you didn't get that speaker enclosure done, too. Had I known, I might have tried to talk you out of selling it. I liked that car."

"I did too, but the guy offered me a good price, and all cash. How do you say no to that?"

"What kid walks in with enough cash to buy a car?" Eliza questioned.

"It wasn't a kid. He was around our age, I'd guess. It was a customer in here a week or so ago. Not one of my regulars." He winked playfully at Eliza, then looked down at Nilah happily eating the chocolate muffin. "He asked about it and got my number. A week later, he sent me a message letting me know he had the money and wanted to buy it. I met him over at the dealership, took his cash, and gave him the keys. I drove out with the Jeep less than an hour later."

Eliza blurted out, "Who would want that car that badly?"

"Hey now. Didn't you just tell me that you would have convinced me to not sell it?"

Backtracking, Eliza said, "I liked the car, Oli. I'm just saying it's weird to put out that much cash that quickly on a modded Integra. I know you took care of it, but it still needs paint."

"Well, it's not my problem anymore," Oliver said. "I was outgrowing it. The next guy can do what he wants with it."

Concerned that the new owner would keep driving recklessly around town with it, Eliza said, "I hope not." She continued by apologizing after remembering how she addressed Oliver when she first walked into the coffee shop. "I'm sorry I came in blaming you. Congrats on the new Jeep. Let me know when you want to lift it." She smirked at Oliver. "Can I get a coffee? I need to get over to the shop. Another busy day."

Oliver filled a large coffee cup and asked, "You have a helper today?" He nodded toward Nilah, now with a face covered in chocolate crumbs.

"Yep. My brother and his wife are stuck out west for another day. A storm parked itself where they are, and some of the roads back are underwater. Nilah's going to help Allie in the store area while I work. Aren't you?" she asked the girl.

Nilah nodded, rubbing her dirty hands together.

Eliza reached for a napkin from the counter and handed it to her niece. She asked Oliver one final question. "What's the damage today?" She pointed at the coffee cup in his hand.

"Nothing. Thanks for checking over the old car and keeping an eye on my driving." He grinned and gave Eliza the hot cup. "Bye, Nilah. It was nice to meet you."

"Bye bye!" Nilah waved with both hands gripping the napkin.

"Thanks, Oli. And sorry again."

CHAPTER 26 - His Clothing

He picked up the phone after it rang, answering with a simple, "Hello?"

"Hi, this is Eric, from Eric's Automotive."

"Oh, uh, hi." Although the walk back to the motel was short, he felt like he had just sat down.

"Hey, so, I found the problem with your Integra."

The words didn't register at first. He was more familiar talking to shops about his SUV. He still had that vehicle sitting in the motel parking lot while he decided if he was keeping it or trying to get both cars back home. But that wasn't his immediate concern. He needed to talk to Eliza. Only after that point would he choose what to do. Once he realized Eric was indeed talking about a car he now owned, he responded, "Oh, right."

"Look, man. I probably should have taken a look before you left. Normally this would be an easy fix, but I see why you had the problem. That hose was really brittle. It was tucked down in the back, so you never would have noticed without looking for it. It's almost amazing you got so much time out of the car before this happened."

He was annoyed. He just bought the car. This wasn't something he had owned for a few years, or over a decade. He paid well over the book value of the car and now it was already in the shop with a busted hose, his fault or not. "Okay?" he replied.

"Long story short, it *is* an easy fix. I just don't have the hose I need on hand. I could band-aid it and all, but I don't know how long it would hold. The hose might break again, and there's not a lot of slack left on it. I should be able to get the part by tomorrow, if you can hold out that long."

Knowing that he had another vehicle, the problem wasn't a lack of transportation. His primary goal was to get back to Eliza's shop. "Tomorrow?" he asked.

"Yeah, man. Tomorrow. It might be late in the afternoon, but by tomorrow. The parts warehouse is a couple hours west. They're usually quick about getting me stuff."

Thinking about the possibility of the band-aid Eric suggested not holding, and him showing up to E's Auto Body and Repair right as the so-called *fix* could possibly fail, he opted for the long-term solution. "Okay. Tomorrow."

"Good. Good. It's not an expensive part. And labor is pretty minimal once I have it. For what it's worth, everything else under the hood looks really good. Whoever's been servicing it knows their stuff."

At least nothing else was going to break right after he got it back. Otherwise, he would have to have a long talk with the owner of the coffee shop.

He replied with the only word he could think of. "Good."

"By the way," Eric started. "I've definitely seen your car around. I always wondered who owned it."

He knew the car wasn't his when Eric saw it before, but he replied as if it was. "Um, right. Thanks."

"Anyway, tomorrow. I'll give you a call when the part comes in."

"Yes. Thanks." He hung up.

Upon realizing he had been out of town for much longer than anticipated, he rummaged through his small suitcase, taking inventory of his clothes. Most were still in acceptable shape to wear again, but what he wore while working on the Integra had acquired some grease stains. He was also afraid that his socks and underwear would soon be standing on their own. The idea of using the same washer and dryer in the motel's facilities with the other guests was repulsive and he hated the thought of going to a laundromat. That would involve waiting around and doing nothing, all to watch his clothes spin in circles.

He remembered seeing signs for a mall nearby. A trip to kill some time and pick up a few more essentials while waiting for the Integra to be fixed seemed like a better idea. Maybe he could find something that would impress Eliza.

He flipped through the racks of clothes in one of the few remaining department stores in the mall, trying to decide what he wanted to wear the next time he was in front of Eliza. He only ever saw her wearing coveralls in her videos. Over the years, a few became increasingly faded before it was evident that she had replaced them with newer ones. Her fingernails had been painted with every shade and tone of the rainbow, leaving him clueless of her favorite color. He made mental notes to ask her about each.

The one time he had been in her immediate presence had nearly been erased from his mind. He could remember leaving the elevator while she lay on the floor, but nothing else. Not what he was wearing, and certainly not what she had on. The trip inside Belinda's Brewpub had him more focused on how her date could meet his demise than her clothing.

While trying to jog his memory to at least recall the color of the shirt she had worn any of those days, he moved from an assortment of button-up dress shirts to jogging sweatpants. With the realization of where he stood, he scolded himself, knowing that arriving at Eliza's automotive shop in leisurewear wouldn't cut it. He was sure that some of her other clientele would show up in tattered and torn clothes, but he thought more highly of himself. *He* would be where her eyes drifted to. Perfect and pristine, like Eliza and her car.

"Hi, there! Can I help you find anything?" a voice greeted him, interrupting his silent cursing.

He looked at the name tag of the person, an obvious indicator that they were an employee of the store. He must have seemed lost or in need of help. "I don't think so," he replied without making eye contact, hoping to be left to his own devices.

"Oh, yeah, okay. Well, I'm Logan. Just give me a shout if you do. I'm quite good at picking out styles to compliment your features. And you, if I may say, do have some nice ones."

Why are they still talking? he thought to himself. *I can do this myself. I don't need any help.*

"I've been told I'm also really good at picking out outfits that make great first impressions. Or continued impressions, if you need to reignite that spark. If you know what I'm getting at." Logan winked as they wandered their way over to the men's boxer briefs and began thoroughly organizing them one at a time.

"First impression?" he asked. He didn't want to engage in the conversation, but he kept speaking. "I want to make a better, um, good, first impression."

"*Dooo* tell." Logan slid their way back over.

While trying to decide how to proceed with the conversation, he pulled out his phone and made an attempt to correct his comment that drew the employee back to him. "I mean, the second one. The spark." He wanted help, and this person seemed to know what to do. "Can—can I show you her?"

"Sure. I'll see what I can work with." Logan started flipping through the clothing on the rack between the two, sorting the items with seeming intent.

He kept his grip on his phone and turned it around so the screen was facing Logan. Peeking at it to make sure it was lit up, he said, "That's her."

"I mean. She seems all right. What can you tell me about her?"

Logan should be more enthused. Eliza is a goddess. "She likes cars."

"Yaaay. So that's what's up with the drab, gloomy blue coveralls? All right, come, I can work with it."

He followed Logan through a few clothing racks in the center of the men's section and ended at a shelf of T-shirts.

"Look, grab one or two of these, a pair of distressed jeans, and—" Logan looked down at the Chuck Taylors on their customer's feet. "It's time to let those go. Our shoes are over that way." Logan pointed toward a sign hanging from the ceiling that said *Shoes*. "Get yourself a pair of nice black boots. Yeah?" Their focus moved up. "The hat should go, too. It hides your face."

He nodded and looked at the selection of T-shirts. They weren't out of the realm of what he sometimes wore, but he thought he'd need something different to impress Eliza. After picking up two shirts that looked like they would fit, he forced a smile at Logan and said, "Thanks."

"No problem. When it doesn't work out, just come back to me. Uh, here. Come back here." Logan made a quick bow and went off.

Once he found a pair of jeans that looked like they had been through war, he chose some other necessities before picking out a pair of black combat boots. He made an effort to find a register far from Logan to pay for the items before leaving the mall.

He headed toward the motel with a few extra sets of clothes, and much-needed underwear, and took a minor detour past Eric's Automotive. A red stop light outside the shop gave him a moment to find his new car. The Integra was still sitting where he had parked it earlier. It *was* nice looking. He began picturing himself driving it with Eliza as a passenger. She was talking to him, telling him how great of a vehicle it was and how she couldn't wait to get her hands on it, and him. Next, seeing himself in Eliza's shop, he was handing her a tool while she was talking to the camera for one of her videos. "After a decade of doing this myself, I now have a partner helping me. Wave hi to everyone—"

A short beep from the vehicle behind him brought his attention back to the road. He saw the light was now green. He cursed loudly at the person interrupting his daydream and shoved the accelerator down to the floor. The motel arrived into sight much quicker than he anticipated.

After unloading his new clothes into his room, he opened his laptop. He navigated to Eliza's webpage and saw a message at the top; a reminder for the live video that she was doing in the evening. Not wanting to risk missing a single minute of what she said, he plugged the power cord for the laptop into the device.

He loaded the most recent prerecorded video and got comfortable, prepared to listen to Eliza's voice. With an alarm set matching the time advertised for her live video, he closed his eyes and tuned his ears to her voice. He nodded along as if she was talking directly to him.

CHAPTER 27 - E's Auto Body and Repair

11 Years Prior

Eliza was standing in front of an empty automotive garage. The sign from the previous owner was tattered and missing letters. She turned to her brother. "Dad never wanted me to be a mechanic. He only wanted to make sure I could handle myself. I don't know that buying my own garage is what he had in mind."

"Li, Dad just wanted you to be happy. You should have seen the joy on his face when you'd still go over to the house and make sure that beat-up truck of his started, even when he couldn't drive anymore. He was so happy to see you out in the driveway following in his footsteps. He wouldn't leave the kitchen window for a minute. I know he wished he was out there with you during those days." Johnny stepped up to the building and ran a hand across the exterior. He looked at his dirty fingertips, then wiped them on his already dirt-covered pants. "This one needs a power washing and some paint, but I think it's better than the last place we looked at. I'll see what I can borrow from a jobsite for you to give it a fresh coat."

"I don't know why he kept it. That truck. It's not like either of us wanted it." The bed of the truck had begun to rust through and a replacement for it cost more than the vehicle was worth.

"I think it was his way of keeping you visiting. After you moved out, he'd still tinker while he could, but never as much as when you were home."

"But I didn't need the truck to be there to go see him. And you still lived there for a while longer." Eliza approached the door of the building and pulled the handle. When it didn't budge, she said, "It was worth a try."

"I know. But it was something that you two did together when we were young. Either way, he'd be really proud of you to do this on your own and not be working for someone else."

"Sure, but Midtown has been good to me. They've given me the experience. I like the other mechanics there. And I definitely don't know how to run a business."

"Look, take your part of the inheritance and do what you want with it, or give it to me. Your favorite brother." Johnny held out his hands, palms down, and moved his fingers in a way to attempt to bewitch Eliza.

"My *only* brother. And in your dreams. I just wish Dad could see this, though." Eliza ran her fingers through her chin-length hair, pulling it up and pausing, before letting it drop back down. "How will I get customers? I'm not going to steal them away from the guys."

"I'm sure you'll find a way. You're savvy on the computer. Make yourself a website. Take some pictures of your car. Show them what you can do."

"But what will I even name it?" Eliza eyed the sign that once said *Jake's Garage*, but now read *e's rage*.

"You have your own name, put it on there. Li's Auto. Eliza's Automotive. Banding's Brakes and Belts." Johnny made sure to spread his hands high and apart each time he offered up a suggestion, as if painting the new logo on the wall for Eliza to see.

"I don't hate that last one." Eliza scratched her chin, thinking about the list, picturing each name on the wall. She wondered how much it would cost to buy a new sign and hoped the number of letters didn't make it cost prohibitive.

"Anyway, put some thought into it. But I really think you should do it. Plus, I expect there to be family discounts." Johnny wiggled his brow.

Eliza shook her head. "John, you know how to do all of this stuff just as well as I do. Dad made you help him, too." Without warning, she started hopping up and down, startling her brother. "Oh my gosh!" she shouted, causing Johnny's eyes to go wide. "Do you remember when that tire started rolling down the hill when you were changing the brake pads? You dropped Dad's favorite C-clamp to go chasing it. I don't know what he was more mad about. The tire hitting the mailbox, or the chips in the red paint of that clamp."

"That wasn't the first time I did something wrong while working with the old man. Anyway, I get paid well enough now to have someone else do it for me." Johnny puffed out his chest.

"Since when do you take your car anywhere near a shop?" she asked skeptically.

Johnny's torso deflated. "Never. I don't trust anyone. But I *would* trust you." He gave Eliza a couple light pats on her back.

Brushing a fake tear away from the corner of her eye, Eliza looked at her brother. "Aw, I love you too."

"Gross. You ruined it."

"All right, fine. I'll do it." Eliza scrunched her face. "Yes. I'll do it. This one right here." She suddenly realized she had no idea how to proceed with actually purchasing a building. "Johnny, do you think that fiancée of yours can help? She knows numbers, right?"

"Lindsay? Yeah. I can ask her. She'd be happy to help. I think she likes you better than me anyway."

Eliza backed away from the building and leaned against the door of her Celica. The midnight blue paint slowly turned to black as the sun continued to set while they stood in the parking lot of the empty automotive garage. She looked back and forth between her cherished vehicle and the building, trying to picture the car parked at its possible new daytime home.

E's Auto Body and Repair, she thought. *That might work.*

CHAPTER 28 - Little Helper

"Hey, Allie. Thanks for getting the shop open this morning," Eliza said while standing in the lobby of her automotive garage.

"Sure thing," came the reply. "I see you brought a helper today. Not trying to replace me, are you?" Allie looked down and smiled at Nilah, who was tightly gripping Eliza's leg.

"Nobody could replace you," Eliza replied. "You remember Nilah? Johnny's daughter."

Allie nodded. "I haven't seen you since you were a baby, Nilah. Your mom and dad brought you into your aunt's shop to show you off in your mini coverall onesie that she bought you when you were born."

Nilah looked up at her aunt. "What are cover alls?"

"They help protect your clothes when you're working," Eliza answered. "They're thick too, so they also protect your body."

A small nod from the young girl let Eliza know that the question had been answered satisfactorily.

"Nilah, I'm going to need you to stay with Allie for some of the day, okay? We have a small TV in the waiting area that you'll be able to watch." Thinking about the content on the screen, usually showing TV programming of trash talk shows or car topics and racing, she added, "Allie can put on some cartoons for you."

Nilah nodded again in response to Eliza's explanation.

"I'll take a break for lunch and we can go get some food together. Does that sound okay?"

"Yes!" Nilah finally replied out loud.

"Al, I'm going to have to work a little late tonight in the shop." Eliza focused on her assistant. "I have that live stream this evening."

The look on Allie's face was enough to know that if there wasn't a young child around, the words that would have left her mouth would have been, "Oh, shit."

"Don't worry. I know you have to leave early," Eliza assured her. She recalled the conversation from the previous week when Allie made sure it was okay that she took off before closing. At the time, Eliza wasn't supposed to still have Nilah with her and was only going to be recording the live video; something that she wouldn't need her assistant around for. "Nilah brought some books and her tablet with her. She'll be okay out here. I'll just be in the room nearby."

"If you're sure," Allie said. "I could cancel and stick around."

"It's not your job to babysit. We'll be fine. Won't we, Nilah?" Eliza pulled the girl in close.

Nilah's eyes were already on the TV in the corner of the room.

"See, we'll be fine." Eliza chuckled.

"Nilah," Eliza called into the lobby from the garage. "Do you want to help me in here for a little bit?"

Allie took her focus away from the customer she was ringing up and cocked her head at Eliza.

Noticing the reaction, Eliza first addressed the man at the counter. "Jay, that squeal should be gone now. You were dead on." She gave the customer an enthusiastic thumbs up. "I got it to happen by giving it some gas going uphill. The belt on the alternator had too much slack so it was slipping. Everything else looked good."

"Thanks, Eliza. I just want to get another year or so out of it," the man replied.

"You shouldn't have a problem with that. I'm pretty sure you could run it without oil for a month and it would be fine." She stopped herself. "Please don't do that." Finally addressing Allie with Nilah now standing in the doorway with her, she said, "I know." She changed her tone to mock her own demeanor and wagged a finger. "*Don't let children into the garage.* But I'm just doing some interior detailing. Nilah's small hands will help."

A smirk from Allie finished the conversation with Eliza before she returned to the customer.

Eliza led Nilah carefully into the garage bay and to the nearest vehicle.

"Aunt 'liza," the girl started.

"Yes?"

"I don't have any cover ons."

"Huh?" She watched Nilah point at the clothes Eliza was wearing. After she thought for a moment, she understood the meaning of the comment. "Oh, cover*alls*?"

Nilah nodded.

"That's okay. We're not going to be doing anything that needs them. But I'll tell you what, I'll try to find a pair that's your size so the next time you're here with me you can wear them. Deal?"

Nilah emphatically nodded in response.

"Great." Eliza looked at the Q60 coupe sitting with its doors wide open; another car brought into the shop strictly for Eliza's attention to detail when it came to doing anything inside or outside of a vehicle. It was the type of work that required time, but not as much hard manual labor as some of the other work she did. Detailing a vehicle was a welcome break where she could crank up the shop's radio and focus on small pieces rather than diagnose large problems. "We're going to clean the inside of that car," she told her niece.

Eliza walked to the vehicle with Nilah close to her side. "I have a hard time fitting in the back seat of a car like this. Maybe you could help me?"

"Yup!"

"I'll give you a cloth and a spray bottle. I just need you to spray some of the cleaner on the cloth, and wipe the sides and the back of these front seats." Reaching into the Q60 to move the front seat forward, she scanned the interior of the vehicle, pleased that it wasn't too messy to begin with. Once Nilah was done wiping down everything, Eliza would be able to reach between the front seats to vacuum the floors, and get to the side crevices through the gap between the door sills and front seats. The more she looked around the inside of the car, the more she wondered why its owner had bothered to bring it to her in the first place. *Easy work*, she thought.

With the Q60's interior freshly cleaned, Eliza stood outside of the vehicle with her small helper. Both admired their handiwork. "Hungry?" Eliza asked Nilah.

"Yes," the girl replied, grinning.

"Let's see if Allie wants us to bring her back anything, and then we can go."

Nilah skipped behind her aunt while they headed to the lobby of the shop.

"Hey, Al," Eliza said.

"Yeah, Boss?" Allie responded.

"I'm running out for food with Nilah. Can I grab you anything?" Eliza almost regretted her word choice as soon as it came out of her mouth. She hoped Allie would refrain from her typical response when given the opportunity to reply with an innuendo, knowing the change in her audience.

"I'll tell you what you can grab me," Allie started.

Eliza began to cover her face before Allie could finish.

"A Caesar chicken wrap from the deli a block over, if you don't mind."

Eliza was surprised, until Allie added one more request.

"And a picture of that sweet, sweet, piece of meat that rings you up."

Sighing in response, Eliza replied with only a thumbs up and ushered Nilah out the door.

CHAPTER 29 - Last-minute Decision

"Nilah, can you get out and go stand by the shop door, please?" Eliza asked as she pulled the car into a typical customer location outside of E's Auto Body and Repair. Earlier in the day, she had discovered that Johnny's CR-V did not fit in her normal tight parking spot while allowing both her and her niece to get out easily. After Nilah did as she was asked and was standing safely out of the way of any moving vehicles, Eliza repositioned the car into her dedicated spot. She joined the young girl who was focused only on the blinking lights of the *Open* sign on the door. "You have your yard to play in at your house, Ni. This is mine." Nilah took in the sight of the fenced-in blacktop parking lot before the two walked inside.

"Here you go, Allie." Eliza handed her employee a wrapped-up food item.

"Dang, girl. Look at those nails. I didn't notice them this morning." Allie grabbed Eliza's hand before she could pull it back and gently forced Eliza's fingers out straight.

"Thanks. They were Nilah's idea."

Allie faced Nilah. "Good job, little girly. Vroom vroom."

"Anyway," Eliza started. "Your piece of *meat* was——" She looked down at Nilah now staring back at her. "Sold out. Unless you like old, shriveled, dried-up meat."

"Sometimes I could go for whatever's available, ya know?" With a wink, Allie laid the chicken wrap on the counter and opened it. She took a bite while exaggerating her "Mmm."

"No. No, I don't." Knowing that the conversation needed to end before Allie slipped up and said something that couldn't be explained away to Nilah, Eliza spoke directly to the young girl. "I need to take care of some things in the garage that I can't have you in there for." She thought about the tools that she needed to move, and the cars that had to be swapped from the lifts before she did her live video. She knew she didn't want to be looking for Nilah underfoot at every turn. "Can you hang out in here with Allie? You can ask her to change the channel on the TV, or maybe you can help her put some of our new merchandise on the shelves."

"What's mer-chances?" Nilah asked.

"Merchandise is the stuff I sell." Eliza stepped close to one of the shelves and pulled off a gauge that was hanging on a hook. She showed it to Nilah. "Stuff like this is what people come in here to buy." She paused to read the label on the package. Looking at Allie, she asked, "Why are we still selling these? Most cars have a voltage gauge built in now."

"Dunno, E. Though someone just bought one the other day. Actually, he had wanted to talk to you after he got it, but you weren't here. It must have been when you took off early on Friday to get Nilah. He said he'd come back. Today maybe. I don't know. I haven't seen him."

Eliza took a look at the time and responded, "Well, if he doesn't come soon, he won't see me today either. I've gotta get everything cleaned up and set up for the video later." Eliza didn't want to intentionally blow off a new client, but she knew she had other priorities to appease her current customers, while possibly bringing in a couple more.

"All right, if he comes in early enough, I'll let you know."

Eliza crouched down to Nilah's eye level and held out the gauge in her hand. "So, this is what merchandise is. Does that make sense?"

Nilah nodded. "Can I watch TV now?"

Replacing the item to the hook on the wall, she made a request of Allie. "Can you find something for her to watch?" Eliza checked the time again. "When do you have to leave?"

"I still don't have to go anywhere. I can stay."

"No, Al. Stop. You need to go."

"Do I have to?"

Eliza answered her friend with an eye roll.

Allie held the TV remote in her hand and pointed it toward her boss. She began mashing down the mute button in a way Eliza could see. After a quick snicker from each, Allie turned toward the TV in the waiting area. She flipped through the channels on the device while adding, "Fine. Just remember I offered."

"Come get me if you need me. I'll be in the garage."

"You always are," Allie shot back playfully.

"Nilah, do you need anything?" Eliza looked toward her niece sitting in one of the plastic chairs and staring up at the TV now showing a cartoon with squirrels. When she received no response, she shrugged toward Allie.

"I got her, E. Go take care of your stuff. I'll holler before I leave."

"Thanks, Al." Eliza left the lobby to finally get back to work in the garage.

After rearranging the cars and clearing out some of the extra junk in the garage, Eliza ran back into the lobby of the shop.

Allie watched her boss take the voltage gauge off of the hook again and caught her before she ran back into the garage. "Wha . . . Whatcha doing?"

"Last-minute change of plans for my video."

"Is that a good idea?"

Knowing that Allie didn't usually question her decisions, she reassured her. "I called the owner. He was only going to do a dual gauge pillar, but I told him I'd add in the extra gauge for free. After I noticed them sitting here earlier, I figured why not." She began tossing the package in the air and catching it. "I've installed a million of these. They're really hard to mess up."

"A million, huh?" Allie raised an eyebrow.

"Hush. At least a dozen." Eliza went over to Nilah to check on the girl. "We'll head back to my home in about an hour and a half or two. Do you still have some snacks in your backpack if you need them?"

Nilah nodded, still focused on the TV.

"Nilah?"

The girl finally turned to look at Eliza. When she noticed who was next to her, she gave her a big hug. "I'm good, Aunt 'liza."

"Great." Eliza returned the hug. She spoke to Allie again, "I need to get back in there. I have a few more things to double check."

"'kay. I'm leaving in about fifteen minutes, I'll let you know."

"Sounds good."

CHAPTER 30 - Tutorial Video 3

"Hey, E," Allie said while walking into the garage bay.

Eliza was in the process of adjusting her camera. She glanced up at Allie. "You out?"

"Yeah, in a few. Unless you need me to stay."

"Just go already."

"Fine, *Mom*. Nilah's good out there. She's playing on her tablet now. I'll let her know when I'm leaving. Want me to lock the door behind me when I go?"

Eliza realized that she would barely have sight of her niece through the garage's window while recording her video. She could periodically look and make sure all was okay, but there would certainly be a few minutes here or there where she wouldn't have a straight view, and Nilah wouldn't be able to see her. Locking the door to get in and out of the shop would be a good idea. "Yes, please."

"You ready?" Allie asked, nodding her head toward the setup in the garage—a camera connected to a laptop with extra lights pointed toward Eliza's makeshift stage, and a purple PPF-wrapped Mustang as her backdrop.

"I hope so. I'm a little nervous about this one." Eliza began walking around the garage, moving different carts one way or the other. She made sure certain ones were out of view of the camera, while others were within her reachable range.

"You'll be fine. You're just talking to the camera like you usually do, right?"

"Yes, but no editing on this one. *When* I drop a tool, I can't edit out when I inevitably say 'shit'." She chuckled at her next thought before she could even say it. "Or, you know, if I burp, I can't take it out later."

"Want me to get you a soda before I leave?" Allie playfully asked. "Maybe even a burrito. Extra beans?"

"Stop. Get out of here. I've only got five minutes left anyway." Eliza motioned for Allie to walk out the door. "Thanks for keeping an eye on Nilah today."

"No problem. She was easy. See you tomorrow, Boss."

"Later, Al."

After one final check of everything around her, Eliza took a deep breath and clicked the button shown on her laptop's display to begin the live video stream. She spent a couple moments looking at the screen while the view back showed herself. A small indicator at the top showed her that there were already two dozen watchers. The number climbed as the next few moments went by, then Eliza finally spoke.

"Hi, all." Her throat went dry. She closed her mouth, trying to will back the moisture and quickly cleared her throat in the process. She thought back to the first video she recorded; a simple tutorial for checking a car tire's air pressure. She was nervous then, but got a welcome surprise when her business picked up over the following couple weeks. Customers came into the shop praising her natural on-camera abilities. Feeling her heart rate slow, her throat began to open back up.

"I'm happy to see so many of you joining me this evening. Tonight, we're going to install a voltage gauge." She picked up the packaging holding the gauge and held it up in front of herself to show her audience. "They're quite simple actually, and we still have a few in stock here at the shop." Eliza immediately regretted not opening the clamshell packaging prior to the start of the video. She leaned over to reach for a nearby pair of scissors and began to slowly and quietly cut the plastic while continuing to talk to the camera. "We just need to find a power line to tap into and a place for ground, which can be any bare-metal spot on the vehicle."

She was talking directly to him. That was the same gauge he bought from her shop, and she was showing him how to install it. He slammed his hand down on the sofa. If he had just waited, she could have shown him how to do it and he may not have damaged his new car.

The Eliza looking at him through his laptop screen continued to make eye contact only with him. He stopped his outburst, not wanting to embarrass himself.

Eliza's voice came through the laptop speakers. "The customer had a dual gauge pod installed on the A pillar prior. They already had a boost gauge and brought in the car for an oil pressure gauge. While thinking about how I wanted to do that, I suggested they add on the voltage gauge. That meant changing to a triple gauge pod, but there are a lot of good ones already made for the Mustang that allow for an easy swap. Here, let me show you."

The view on the screen in front of him displayed Eliza getting closer as her arm reached out. He eyed the intricate details painted on her fingernails. One appeared to have a tiny car on it. The view suddenly moved, seeming to float into the driver side of the Mustang. It showed a loosely-fit triple gauge pod with two holes filled in and one empty. Realizing that he was seeing the inside of the car from Eliza's point of view, he felt like it was his hand with painted nails pointing to the empty spot. Eliza's disembodied voice announced, "We'll put the voltage gauge here."

Trying her best to not get tangled in the cord running between the camera in her hand and the laptop, Eliza kept the motion slow while returning the camera to its dedicated spot on the table. She wanted to avoid giving her viewers motion sickness.

"This kit didn't give me the amount of wiring I needed, so what you'll want is at least a few extra feet of 16-gauge wire. I'm going to tap into the fuse panel that's over on the passenger side for my 12-volt source, and for ground I'll run a wire down behind the kick plate on the driver side." Eliza picked up a small coil of red wire and unwound it. "I precut what I needed, giving myself an extra two feet of slack that I'll trim off before connecting it. But this way, I'm not trying to tuck a full spool of wire behind panels while working in tight places."

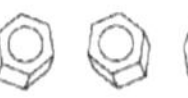

Eliza's hands extended past the edges of his screen as she was now holding out a black wire that was slightly shorter than the red wire she previously had.

So as to not miss any of the video, he picked up his pen and paper where he was keeping notes. He planned to type them into his expanding document collection of information about Eliza's videos. At the top of the paper, he had written the date with the title *Eliza Live*. On the next available line, he wrote *Eliza out of frame*. He wasn't sure if this would be his only chance to see this video before he would inevitably meet with Eliza. He needed to know every specific detail so he could show her how well he listens to her.

With the paper and pen replaced to their spot next to him on the sofa, he continued to follow Eliza's motions.

"I'm sorry to have to move the camera around again, but I want you to be able to see what I'm doing," the on-screen Eliza said.

You don't have to be sorry, he thought. *About anything. Everything you do is perfect.*

The image moved to the inside of the Mustang again, but from a viewpoint from the rear seats looking forward. It allowed for a limited perspective of the center console. The screen flickered, changing to a fisheye view of the car's cabin. He could now see the entire front of the vehicle's interior, including both doors. Eliza climbed in from the passenger side and began speaking.

"I'm going to pop off these few panels here so I can access the fuse box."

Eliza disappeared from view. Shortly after, her body showed up in frame on the driver side.

"And I'll remove these panels here, where I'll attach the ground wire."

CHAPTER 31 - Coming Home

"I still haven't gotten through to Eliza yet." Johnny ended the attempted call and placed his phone on his lap.

With the steering wheel in her hand, and her eyes on the road, Lindsay said, "Doesn't she have that video tonight?" She delivered a sideways glance and a small smirk. "Don't you pay attention to anything your sister does? Stop bugging her." The bridge that led out of the area was no longer underwater, allowing them to head home. Lindsay knew Johnny had tried calling once when they first left, and again after they switched seats for the remainder of the commute. "We'll be home in a couple of hours."

"Yeah, I know, but I wanted to let her know we were on our way," Johnny said.

"Nothing between now and then will change if your call does or doesn't go through."

"Yeah, I guess. I just figured we could say hi to Nilah too while we're on the way."

"Why don't you watch some of Eliza's thing?" Lindsay asked. "Keep yourself occupied."

"You mean, stop bugging you while you're driving?" Johnny laughed. "I'm almost too nervous on her behalf to do that."

"Just support your sister. The extra viewers can't hurt."

"Fine." Johnny picked up his phone again and navigated to Eliza's webpage of videos. He found the link at the top to open the live stream. He tapped it and waited a moment for the video to load. Eliza's voice came through the tiny speakers.

"While I'm on this side, I'll pop the gauge into its new home at the bottom of the gauge pod," Eliza said.

Looking at his sister addressing her viewers from the inside of a two-door coupe, Johnny could just make out the logo of a running pony on the steering wheel. "Is she wearing makeup?" he asked.

Lindsay took a quick glance in Johnny's direction, then returned her eyes to the road. She smacked her husband on the leg with the back of her hand.

"Ouch, what?"

"I'm sure she just wanted to cover up what remains of that bruise. I know she tries to hide it with her hair, but that won't help when she's moving around so much."

Johnny watched Eliza on his small screen contort her body to run a wire from the voltage gauge to the passenger side of the car. Her head was nearly upside down, and her hair was hanging low. "True," was the best he could muster.

In the position she was now in, Eliza was happy to be wearing coveralls. There was no worry about her shirt rising up and exposing her midsection on the live video. However, she wished she had put her hair in a ponytail. It would be easier to move her hair from underneath herself while she twisted her body to shove the wire down a small gap.

"By the way," she said loudly with the back of her head to the camera. "Make sure to disconnect the positive lead from the battery before doing anything power related in a vehicle. Twelve volts isn't a lot, and the amperage isn't that high, but it's better safe than sorry."

While pushing herself out of the car from the passenger side, she reached for the camera. "Let me show you where I ran the positive wire."

He couldn't believe how easy Eliza was making the installation of the voltage gauge look. If he would have known that he didn't have to run the wire into the engine bay, and directly to the battery, he would have been at Eliza's shop *now*. Maybe he could have been helping her during this video. His larger frame wouldn't allow him to contort the way she was in tight spaces, but he was sure there was something he could do to assist. He slammed his fist into the couch again, causing his pen to bounce off and land on the floor.

While reaching down to pick it up, he missed when the small figure first walked into the frame.

"Can I help?" came the voice of a young girl. Her face was obscured by the body of the car.

A dozen questions ran through his head. *She has a daughter? Why didn't I know that? Why didn't she tell me? That's okay*, he thought. *I love kids.* He enjoyed spending time with his nephew—the few times he got to see him when he and his brother were on speaking terms. He would love to play games with the girl. Show her the things he enjoyed, such as watching her mom on the screen. Maybe he could go over to the shop after the video was finished. *How much time was left?* he wondered. He guessed about twenty minutes. He could drive over there as soon as it was done and Eliza and the girl would probably still be there.

"Excuse me one moment, please," a rattled Eliza said. "My assistant-in-training just joined us. We'll be right back after these messages."

He watched Eliza step off the screen, leaving a view of the Mustang's dash. Through the front windshield, he could make out Eliza's large tool boxes lining the wall, with a few automotive posters hung above them.

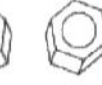

"Nilah," Eliza whispered. "I need another fifteen or twenty minutes, okay? Then I'll be done."

Eliza walked Nilah back into the lobby of the shop, sitting the young girl down in front of the TV.

"Okay," Nilah responded. She looked down toward her feet. "I wanted to help like before."

"I know, but I'm sorry. Next time, all right?"

"Okay. Can we play a game when you're done?"

"Sure, Ni. We can play a game. I'll be back."

Eliza made sure Nilah was sitting in place before she rushed back into the garage.

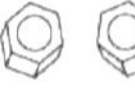

"Was that Nilah?" Lindsay laughed, her hands sliding around the steering wheel as she prepared to turn.

"You know it. She can't make anything easy for anyone, can she?" Johnny said. "You could only see her shirt, the puppy one. Not her face. But we know that voice anywhere."

"I wonder if she's worn anything but that shirt since we left. I don't know why we bothered packing anything else for her." Lindsay checked the side mirrors before moving over to take the next exit off the highway.

"I hope Eliza has made her shower at least once while we were gone," Johnny said.

"We'll be able to tell well enough by the smell once we get her."

Johnny waved at the air in front of his nose, as if he was already standing near his daughter. "How do kids smell so bad?"

Eliza quickly composed herself, trying to remember what step she left off at before stepping back into view of the camera.

"As I was saying," she began, not skipping a beat. "I ran the positive wire to the fuse box." She sat in the driver side of the Mustang and pointed toward the passenger side. "Now I'll connect the negative wire. The black one."

Eliza picked up the uncoiled wire. While holding one end in one hand, she reached behind the loose gauge pod with her other hand to push the second lead from the gauge out to the side. "First, I'll connect these two ends together to give me a longer amount of wire to work with." She reached blindly into the cup holder next to her. The wire nut she expected to find wasn't there. The bright yellow plastic piece was visible on the floor of the passenger side. After a deep breath to remain calm and continue to keep her language clean, she leaned over the center console and picked up the part she needed. Holding the two wires together in one hand, she twisted the wire nut over the two pieces of bare metal.

She turned her head slightly toward the camera while finishing tightening the nut. "Sometimes I solder these, but inside a car this perfect I don't want to risk small splatters of molten lead ruining anything. These wire nuts will hold tight, and I'll wrap some electrical tape over it for good measure."

Eliza leaned out of the car and picked up a black roll of electrical tape. She cut off a small strip and wound it tight around the two connected wires and wire nut.

His phone rang while he was still focused on the laptop screen. He continued watching Eliza finish the installation of the voltage gauge. She turned the key in the ignition of the Mustang and pointed out that the new gauge registered slightly over twelve volts. The phone continued to ring, masking some of Eliza's words. Frustrated by the interruption, he pushed the button on the phone to silence the call. Nothing was important enough to cause him to miss a minute of Eliza talking in real time.

"And that will about do it," Eliza said. "I hope that helps some of you for when you want to install a gauge like this. This information can be used on any number of modifications that need twelve volts. Switches and interior lights are good examples." The Eliza on his display reached toward him and the view began to float out from the interior of the car. The screen now showed the outside of the Mustang from the same position as when the video started.

"Let me know in the comments if I should do another live video in the future and what topic I should cover. Until next time, I'm Eliza at E's Auto Body and Repair, right at the corner of West Victoria and Chestnut."

Eliza's arm reached toward him one more time and the video went black.

His hand was out waiting to accept hers when she disappeared. He blinked and looked around, realizing that he was alone.

His phone lit up, catching his attention from the corner of his eye. It showed that he had received a voicemail. Not focusing completely on it, he tapped the button to make the message play.

"Hey, look, uh." There was a pause in the voice coming from the small device. "The part for your Integra didn't get here today. Something about some roads being flooded. I'm really sorry, man. At best, it'll be here tomorrow and I can take care of it first thing. I hope you can wait another day. Oh, right, uh, this is Eric. Sorry aga—"

He pushed the button to stop the message before it completely finished. He grabbed the keys to his other vehicle from the end table and headed toward the door of his motel room.

CHAPTER 32 - Hide and Seek

Eliza took a deep breath. She looked around the garage, then down at the camera and the laptop it was connected to.

"That was all right," she said to herself. "I didn't mess up anything too badly. The install went well. The car is still in one piece." The key for the Mustang was sitting on the dash in the vehicle. She reached in and grabbed it. As she stood, she closed the driver side door, satisfied with the solid thunk it made as it latched shut. Swinging the keychain around her finger, she headed toward the lock box where she stored her customers' keys. She hung the Mustang's fob on an empty hook and closed the lock box for the night.

Eliza returned to the table holding the laptop and camera. She noticed a few comments had begun to pop in under the empty video box on the computer's screen. She closed the laptop lid, knowing that they could wait for another time and that she needed to check on her niece. Eliza left the garage bay and headed to the lobby of her shop.

"Nilah," she called. "I'm done now. Are you ready to go?"

Before making it to the young girl, Eliza stopped at the entrance door. She jiggled the handle and checked that the *Open* sign had been turned off. She unlocked the door in preparation for them to leave.

"I'm ready," Nilah answered, keeping her eyes focused on the TV while acknowledging that her aunt was talking to her.

Continuing to where her niece was sitting, Eliza gave the young girl a small pat on the head and turned off the TV. The flicker of the screen going black caused

Eliza to remember that she wanted to take her laptop with her. "Ni, I'll be right back. I forgot something, okay? Can you pack up your stuff?"

"Okay," Nilah replied. "I will."

Eliza began to walk away before Nilah asked her a question.

"Aunt 'liza, is this place smaller and with less people?"

The question stopped Eliza in her tracks. "Smaller than what?" she asked.

"Than the zoo."

Not understanding the purpose of the question, she answered plainly. "It's just us, Nilah. And it's pretty small, sure. I'll be right back, okay?"

"This is small enough?"

Eliza wanted to get her computer so they could go. "Yes. It's small."

"At least ten," Nilah said, more as a demand than a request or question.

"Probably only for ten seconds. I'll be fast." Eliza started moving toward her destination.

"Okay!"

After entering the garage, Eliza grabbed the laptop and did a once-over to make sure nothing would stop her from getting right back to work when she returned in the morning. She tried to reach for her phone, but her coveralls were in the way of her shorts pockets and she couldn't get to it. In the struggle to get the work clothing down low enough to get her hand on the device, she knocked a box of wrenches off of a wheeled cart. The clatter of metal on the concrete floor filled the unusually quiet room. When the shop was open, the sound would have blended in with blaring music and running air compressors. She normally wouldn't have flinched, but did this time. She scratched at her ears, trying to rub out the ringing that sounded like a bell inside her head. Once she returned the tools to their appropriate place, she retrieved her phone. A few missed calls and a message took up most of the screen.

"All from Johnny," she said. She read the message that had come in a few minutes prior telling her she could ignore the calls.

We're a little over thirty minutes out. We enjoyed the video and the cameo by Ni, too. See you at your place.

A young girl walked out the main entrance of the shop as he sat in his SUV in the lot of E's Auto Body and Repair. He put his phone on the seat next to him after adding a comment to Eliza's newest video. The groan of his clothing rubbing across the worn leatherette seats echoed in the cabin as he slid down, hoping not to be seen. He had worked up the courage to talk to Eliza, to tell her how much her new video would have helped him, and how he wished he was there in his new Integra to show her. With the *Open* sign off, but the inside lights still on, he imagined catching her as she walked out the door. He would stop her in the parking lot of the shop to endlessly discuss many automotive topics, however she wasn't the first person to leave the building.

Eliza's Supra wasn't parked where it always was. In its place was a vehicle that reminded him of his own. The girl that walked out of the shop was wearing the same shirt as the one that appeared in Eliza's live video, so Eliza had to still be in the building.

Peering over the bottom ledge of the window, he watched curiously as the girl slinked around the parking lot. She stepped behind a trash can outside of a garage bay door, her head clearly visible and looking around. From there, she rounded the corner of the building and stayed out of sight for a few seconds before coming back out and wiping at the front of her shirt, an attempt to remove something that could have been dust or spiderwebs.

As dusk began to set, he couldn't see where the girl's eyes were pointed, only that her head was facing in his direction. He slid further down into the seat, completely obscuring his view out the window. He heard a light scraping on the rear door of his vehicle. "Go away," he whispered. The door opened with a creek as it slowly settled into the first notch that kept it from swinging fully open. He held his breath and closed his eyes. The door shut with a light click. He peeked ahead of himself with one squinted eye. The door didn't close enough to turn off the dome light, but at least he was protected.

"Hi! I'm hiding," a voice behind him said. "You're in my daddy's car. You must know him. Who are you? Where's my car seat? Did it need to get cleaned?"

He didn't answer. An opportunity had presented itself. The key was still in the ignition of the vehicle. He turned it to start the SUV, shifted the vehicle into drive, and tapped on the accelerator. After the car lurched forward, he switched his foot to the brake pedal. *No, that won't work.* With the vehicle stopped again, he glanced back at the young girl who was now reaching to latch the seat belt.

"She will never be able to find me," the voice in the back seat said. A giggle followed the words.

Another wave of encouragement flooded him. He turned his focus ahead. *But it might.* His foot moved back to the accelerator. It hovered momentarily before dropping slowly and pushing the pedal down with it. *It will. It has to.* With the car moving once again, he turned the steering wheel to drive the vehicle out the gates of the auto body shop. *I'll be a hero.*

CHAPTER 33 - The Best Spot

Eliza rushed out of the garage, calling to Nilah excitedly as soon as she opened the door. "Ni, your parents are almost home. Let's get out of here so we beat them back." She went to the TV area and looked over the back of the chairs, expecting to see Nilah laying across them. Finding the chairs empty, she called out again. "Nilah?" Eliza went to the single bathroom door. She knocked, hating the automatic closing door that meant she never knew when someone was in there. When she received no response, she opened the door, discovering the room dark and empty. "Nilah, where are you?"

Seeing and hearing no evidence of the young girl, she yelled out once more. "Nilah!" The dread in her voice floated in the air with the name of her niece.

Eliza thought back to the last couple of questions Nilah had asked before she returned to the garage bays. *Smaller place? At least ten? She meant count to ten, didn't she?*

"Hide and seek!" Eliza blurted out. "Nilah, I give up. Come out, come out, wherever you are." The lobby of the shop wasn't large. She looked in every hiding place, including behind the counter where Allie usually stood. *I was in the garage. I would have noticed if she came in there. She wouldn't have gone outside. She couldn't go outside. Allie locked the door when she left.* A thousand thoughts ran through her head as she walked to the entrance of the shop and leaned on the door. When it gave way, she panicked. Eliza suddenly remembered unlocking the door only moments earlier, thinking that she and Nilah were on their way out. She had returned to the garage for the laptop that she was now holding under her arm in little time.

Eliza burst through the door and out onto the blacktop of her shop's parking lot. A short distance ahead, she saw a vehicle that looked like Johnny's driving away. Its lights were off, even though it was beginning to get dark. Eliza wondered if Nilah had gotten the keys and managed to take the car. There had been articles in the news recently of kids younger than her driving away in their parents' car. She turned to face the side of her shop, dreading the thought of finding the single parking spot empty. She was reluctantly relieved when she saw the vehicle parked where she left it. Nilah hadn't taken the car, but Eliza's worry was building.

"Nilah!" she yelled out. "We have to get home. Your mom and dad will be there soon to pick you up. Don't you want to see them?" Eliza looked around the lot, trying to picture where she would hide if she was a young girl. The trash can near the garage bay was too small. Nothing but spiders lived on the far side of the shop, but she knew she should check anyway. Rounding the corner and finding it empty, Eliza returned to the front lot of the shop. She walked to Johnny's car and tried the door handles. The beep that greeted her as her hand hit the handle told her that the doors had been locked. She opened it anyway and peered inside.

"Nilah?" she called softly, not wanting to hurt the young girl's ears if she had managed to get inside the small space. After receiving no response, she faced the parking lot and yelled her niece's name as loud as she could. "Nilah!"

Eliza returned to the inside of the shop. She ran through every square foot, turning over boxes too small to hide a mouse in hopes of finding Nilah. Hysteria started to overtake her as she came to terms that Nilah was nowhere to be found. Her anxiety hung in the air with the words she used as she continued to call for her niece. Tears started to fall and her knees began to buckle.

Eliza's phone rang. "Oh, God. It's probably Johnny."

She fumbled in her pocket, trying to remove the device. Through blurry vision, she could make out enough of the letters to decipher the caller ID: *Police Dept.*

"I need help!" she yelled into the phone receiver before it even made it to her ear.

"Ms. Banding?" the other end asked. "I wanted to let you— Are you okay?"

"No." Struggling with her breathing, Eliza had to gasp for air in between words. "I can't." She took a labored breath in. "Find." Eliza let out a breath. "Nilah."

"Ms. Banding? This is Officer Chapel."

"I need." Eliza choked. "Help."

"Ms. Banding, where are you?"

"My." She fought out a cough. "Shop."

"Ms. Banding, I'm sending someone over there now. Stay on the phone with me, okay?"

"Nilah!" Eliza screamed as she fell to her knees. Her tears fully escaped, rolling down her cheeks and dotting the light gray shirt tucked into her folded down coveralls.

CHAPTER 34 - Police

"Where did you see her last?" the woman in the uniform asked Eliza.

"Inside my shop," she responded, standing in the parking lot of her automotive repair shop. The police officer had arrived minutes after she hung up with Officer Chapel. Eliza speculated that the woman had been in the area on patrol and received the call directly from her supervisor. In an attempt to keep her emotions from spilling out in her words, Eliza kept her arms crossed tightly against her body and pointed an elbow toward the entry door of the building.

"Do you have any reason to believe she would run away?" the officer asked while writing the previous answer in a small notebook.

Eliza could only shake her head as she held herself tighter. Blotchy red streaks lined her cheeks. Nilah would *never* run away from her. Eliza loved her niece and her niece loved her back. Sure, she probably missed her mom and dad, but they would be home soon.

"Sometimes kids run away, even if—"

"She didn't run away!" Eliza snapped at the officer.

"Calm down, Ms. Banding. I need to ask these questions." The officer responded with no hint of emotion. "Do you have a recent picture of the child?"

Eliza thought for a moment before remembering she had taken a picture of Nilah while at the zoo. She held up a finger to the officer while fishing her phone out of her pocket. As she was scrolling through the images from the weekend, a second police car pulled into the lot, interrupting the accusatory questions Eliza felt she was receiving. A large man stepped out of the driver side of the vehicle while it was still rocking from the jolted stop.

The deep voice that was now immediately recognizable to Eliza said, "Ms. Banding. I'm sorry about your niece. We'll do everything we can to locate her." He pointed toward the building. "Can we go inside?"

Eliza nodded her head slightly and began walking to the door of the shop. Officer Chapel, moving quicker than Eliza expected, jumped ahead and pulled the door open. He gestured for Eliza to go in first. Once inside, she nearly collapsed against the shop counter. The bright lights of the lobby cause her to squint through her teary eyes.

The last twenty minutes felt like an eternity. Johnny called while she was still on the phone with Officer Chapel. After rushing the officer off, assuring him that she would remain at the shop, she was finally able to talk to her brother. Johnny sensed the worry in her voice as soon as the line was open, especially when she didn't call him by any playful names and only answered with "John." Eliza could hardly get any words out beyond "sorry" after telling him Nilah was missing. Johnny told her that they had been slowed down in traffic but would be at the shop as soon as possible. Lindsay was in the background crying.

"Ms. Banding," Officer Chapel said to get Eliza's attention. "We *will* find your niece. I was going to tell you this on the phone, but under the circumstances, I wanted to come and tell you in person." He made sure Eliza was focused on him before he continued. "We found some information about your attacker. I know the timing of this isn't ideal, but we may have a short window to act."

Eliza's head lifted slightly as she began to understand what the officer said.

"We found out why he was in that building. He has a friend who lives there. Unfortunately, your attacker does not reside in this state, so it took us longer to track them down. We believe this was a random attack and we don't expect them to be back, but—"

"What does he drive?" she blurted out, hoping the officer had more information than simply where they lived. It was a question she asked out of habit. Any time a person, new or old, was mentioned to her, she asked what they drove. The answer would give her an idea of who the person was, if she had seen the car before, and possibly put a face to the driver.

"What does he— What?" The officer was clearly confused by the question, likely expecting one related to the suspect's name or their address. "It's a—" He pulled out a notebook and flipped through it. "A Santa Fe. Silver."

Eliza was familiar with a lot of vehicles, but a basic SUV wasn't going to get her any more information than being told that the man lived on Earth.

Office Chapel's finger moved across the page in the notebook. Finding another item to mention, he said, "And an Integra coupe that they registered temporarily in this state just this week."

Finally, a car she knew well, and a model she knew was becoming few and far between. Eliza's eyes lit up. "Where did they buy it?"

"I don't—"

"What color is it?"

"Ms. Banding, I—"

"Who did they buy it from?" Immediately remembering that Oliver had just sold his vehicle last week, she needed to know the answer to the question.

"We don't know that. I'm sorry."

The information about her attacker had momentarily distracted her from what was most important. At the realization she said softly, "My niece."

The officer who had been asking Eliza questions outside entered the shop, followed by a man and a woman. "These two say they're the girl's parents," the officer said.

Eliza rushed over to Johnny and Lindsay, throwing her arms around each and burying her head in between their bodies. "I'm so sorry."

Johnny grabbed Eliza gently by the shoulders and guided her upright. "You looked everywhere for her?"

Eliza nodded, recalling the earlier conversation where she told Johnny that Nilah was missing and had wanted to play hide and seek.

"She *is* really good at hiding," he said, strained but hopeful.

"Everywhere, John. *Everywhere.* Inside and out."

"Nilah!" Lindsay frantically called.

"Ms. Banding," the woman officer said, facing Eliza. "We need any other information you can provide about the girl so we can help."

An exhausted Eliza turned to the woman in the uniform.

"What do you remember from when you first couldn't find the girl?"

"I looked everywhere inside." She remembered running through the small area, knowing that there weren't a lot of places to hide. "Then I came outside. A car was driving away. I thought it was my car. My brother's car. I thought Nilah may have tried to drive it."

A brief chuckle came from Johnny before he cleared his throat and the smile quickly faded. "Sorry. She's so small." He returned to nervously wringing his hands.

"And what kind of car is that?" the officer asked.

"A CR-V. But it wasn't his car. It was a silver—"

"A silver what, Ms. Banding?" The officer's nose was in her notebook, waiting for the last piece of information so she could add it to the page.

Eliza's eyes darted back and forth as she replayed several scenes in her head. A silver SUV parked next to her Supra at Grinded Beans. Another pulling into Belinda's Brewpub as she rushed to meet with Lindsay's coworker. And finally, the same vehicle driving away from her shop. What was only background noise before was now suddenly at the forefront of her mind.

"A Santa Fe!"

CHAPTER 35 - Still Hiding

The young girl in the back seat of his car kept talking, distracting him from putting together clear enough thoughts on his plan.

"And then we went to the zoo where I saw monkeys." She put up one finger at a time, counting something or ticking off a list of items.

The sign for the motel slowly crept into view as he drove drastically under the speed limit. He wasn't supposed to have driven this far and it never took him this long to drive between the shop and his short-term housing. He looked into the back seat again and then toward the motel as it neared.

"Next, we went to the mall. You know my Aunt Eliza, right? If you know my daddy, then you have to know my aunt. She's the best. We had so much fun. I don't think she'll *ever* be able to find me."

The name caused a flicker of life in his mind, but with the current happenings, it didn't immediately register. "Aunt?" he asked, not to anyone in particular. "Who?"

"Aunt 'liza!" the girl answered. "I'm playing hide and seek in her auto motif store."

"Shit," he said.

"We don't say that word. It means poopy." His passenger giggled.

Eliza was this girl's aunt. Not her mother. That's okay though, he thought. He still enjoyed kids. His idea could still work. "What's your name?" he asked.

"Nilah," the girl answered. "But you should know that if you know my daddy. I'm sure he talks about me all the time."

"I don't know your dad." The words left his mouth before he could think about their repercussions.

"You don't know my daddy? Then why are you driving his car? And why did you take out my car seat? Is it in the trunk?"

He could hear the panic forming in her voice.

"I want to go back. I think the game is over. I want my aunt. I want my mom. I want my dad." Nilah began kicking the seat in front of her. "Aunt Eliza!"

The motel parking lot had already passed as he kept the car moving at a slow, steady pace.

"I want to go back now." Nilah was starting to get louder. "My daddy will, will—" Panic was starting to turn to fear, with tears and sniffles following.

"I—" He looked for the next turn he could make to get the car turned around and headed back. He knew it hadn't been very long since he left the parking lot of the shop. "I'm going—"

The sign for the motel was now on the other side of the car as he made the return trip. He knew exactly what he would do. "*We're* going back," he announced with excitement.

He would park the car a few buildings down. He wouldn't be seen driving *that* vehicle. Not now. Then he'd walk the girl back to E's Auto Body and Repair. He would proudly tell Eliza that he found the girl wandering. Eliza would invite him into the shop and thank him profusely. Later, he would retrieve the Integra and return with it. She wouldn't be able to resist him. A hero and an automotive enthusiast. What more could she want?

With his plan at the helm, he pushed the accelerator down further.

"All right, Ms. Banding," Officer Chapel said. "We'll put out a notice on the silver Santa Fe, but for now I'll stay here with you in case the girl comes back, okay?"

Looking over at Lindsay, who was sobbing with her arms wrapped around Johnny, Eliza nodded in response to the officer.

"The parents should return to their house in case the girl decides to go there."

"Nilah has been staying with me. She doesn't know that her parents are back yet," Eliza responded.

"Then maybe they should go to your place and wait."

"John," Eliza called to her brother. "Can you guys go over to my apartment and make sure Nilah doesn't go there?" She tried to sound more reassured by that possibility than she believed herself. Nilah couldn't have walked the several hours needed to get there. It wasn't a long distance, but the girl was young.

"Shouldn't we be out looking for her?" Johnny asked. "She would know our voice."

Lindsay tried to answer in agreement, but could only let out weak sobs.

"Let's just keep to her familiar settings," Officer Chapel replied. "Ms. Banding can remain at her shop. I, and the other officers, will be out looking for her. Why don't you keep an eye on the other known place she has been recently?"

Johnny nodded while rubbing Lindsay's back, an attempt to console his wife.

"I'll text you the code to get in." Eliza pulled out her phone and selected Johnny's name. She entered the four numbers needed to unlock the keypad she had installed on her apartment door only days prior, and sent the message.

"Let me know if you find out anything else, Li." Johnny started ushering Lindsay to the door.

"Of course. Tell me if she's at my place?" Eliza still knew the likelihood of Nilah making it all the way to her apartment was slim, but she wanted to be hopeful that the girl was safely on her own and not with someone else.

The thumbs up Johnny managed to show while still wrapped up in Lindsay's grip answered Eliza well enough.

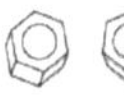

It was nearly dark, but under the streetlights, he could make out the unmistakable form of two police cars in the parking lot of E's Auto Body and Repair as the shop came into view.

"Shit," he said.

"Poopy," Nilah replied. She let out another small giggle, no longer showing fear of being with a stranger after he promised he was taking her back to her aunt.

His makeshift plan had already failed. He wasn't going to risk an interaction with the police. They would think he knowingly took the girl. He wasn't a kidnapper, he told himself, and he didn't want them to think otherwise. Any confrontation with the authority figures would paint him in a bad light to Eliza, and that was not something he was willing to risk. No one was going to stand between him and her.

He took the next turn, changing his direction to avoid passing by the auto shop.

"Are we back yet?" the girl asked.

"It's, uh——" Maybe she hadn't realized they were right there. "I forgot how to get back," he lied. "It's too dark. I can't see?" He waited for the girl to acknowledge him. He couldn't quite tell how old she was and if she would call out his bluff or be able to get to the shop herself.

"Oh. Okay. I don't know how to get there either."

Somewhat relieved, but still not sure what to do with his passenger, he again pointed his car toward the motel. "How about we wait until morning?" He needed more time to think. He still didn't want the girl with him, but didn't know what to do without getting himself in trouble. "We can go back when it's daylight again."

"I'm hungry," Nilah said.

He remembered that he had seen vending machines outside the motel. He proudly said, "We'll get some food, okay?"

The young girl yawned before answering him. "Okay."

CHAPTER 36 - Oliver

"Who did you sell your car to?" Eliza yelled into the speaker of her phone.

"What?" Oliver questioned from the other end of the line.

"Who bought your Integra?"

"I don't know. Some guy." Oliver was audibly confused. "I thought we already talked about this. He came into the coffee shop, asked about the car, and bought it later. He was from out of town, I haven't heard from him since."

Eliza paused momentarily to think. "Do you have his number?"

"Yeah, I do, why? Trying to buy it back from him?" Oliver's chuckle annoyed Eliza.

"He has Nilah!"

"What? What do you mean?" There was a long pause before he added, "Your niece?"

Sitting in the lobby of her shop, Eliza quickly gave Oliver a recap of the events from the last hour. Officer Chapel was still wandering around the building, half looking for Nilah while appearing to be shopping at the same time, but obviously listening to the conversation Eliza was having.

"Are you sure?" Oliver asked. "Why would he have her? That doesn't make any sense. He seemed nice enough, a little agitated during some of the purchase, but didn't act like a kidnapper. He's probably not even in the area anymore."

"We saw his other car. I *think* I saw his other car leaving here after I couldn't find Nilah." She began to second-guess herself, but felt confident in what she saw.

"He, he——" Eliza knew she hadn't told Oliver about the attack in her old apartment building and what she had just learned from Officer Chapel.

"How do you know this? Look, Eliza, I believe you think that, but it seems like a stretch. How do you know he didn't sell the other car? Wouldn't he be driving the Integra? If you didn't want me to sell the car, you should have——"

"He hurt me."

There were a few moments of silence on the other end of the line before Oliver finally asked, "How?"

First starting with the attack in the elevator, and why she had moved, Eliza finally got to the part where the police had told her who they believed the attacker was, and what vehicles they owned.

"So that's where the bruise is from? I assumed you did that in your garage."

Eliza tugged at the hair near her right eye while waiting for Oliver to continue.

"If anyone's going to be able to pick out a random vehicle on the road, it's you." Oliver meant to be serious in his comment; a praise toward Eliza's knowledge of all things with four wheels. "What can I do to help?"

"We need the number of the person that bought your car." Eliza recalled one of Oliver's earlier comments. "If he sold his other car, we need to know who bought it, but either way, I need to talk to that bastard."

"Yeah, sure, hold on one second while I get it."

Eliza heard rustling as Oliver pulled the phone from his ear to begin using it to look for the contact information she wanted. After what felt like an eternity, she heard her phone ding, indicating that she had received a message. Taking a momentary glance at the screen to see that it did indeed come from Oliver, she replaced the device back to her ear, waiting for Oliver to talk again.

"It's sent."

"Yeah, I got it already, thanks."

"Let me know if I can do anything else," Oliver said. "I'll keep an eye out for my car, er, my old car, and what else?"

"A Santa Fe. It looks like my brother's car that I had at your store earlier."

"Oh, yeah, right, okay. I'm sorry again. Good luck."

"Thanks, Oli."

His phone began to vibrate in his pocket as he was feeding dollar bills into the vending machine outside his motel room door. After finally getting the bill acceptor to take the crumbled paper, he pulled out the device and looked at the screen.

"What the hell does he want?" he asked himself, seeing the contact listed as the person he bought the Integra from. Pushing the button to stop the vibration, but not hanging up on the incoming call, he debated answering just to complain about having to take the car into the shop right after buying it. The thunk of the food hitting the bottom of the vending machine reminded him that there was a hungry and tired little girl sitting on the bed in the room. He returned the phone to his pocket and reached for the candy bar. For good measure, he also bought bags of chips and trail mix to provide the girl choices. He wanted her to tell Eliza how accommodating he was.

He took the variety of food into his room, finding Nilah curled up on the bed and asleep. He sighed in relief, knowing that the barrage of questions would be done for the night.

His phone began vibrating again. Assuming it was the Integra's former owner a second time, he blindly reached in his pocket and stopped the call. He wasn't going to risk waking the child.

Quietly making his way to the room's sofa, he sat down slowly, knowing the springs would groan under his weight. He took the candy bar, first holding it off to the side to shield any noises from the wrapper while opening it, then took a bite. A glimmer of light peeking between the curtains of the room's back window caught his eye. He hadn't opened them once since arriving, and had no idea what was on the other side.

Standing carefully to limit any noises from the couch, he went to the back of the motel room and peeked out the curtains. He found a full moon illuminating the entire area, revealing what appeared to be two separate lakes and a park with a playground. The light from the moon reflected off the water and back at him, causing him to squint. After he checked the lock on the window to make sure it couldn't be opened, he backed away, pulling the curtain tight to keep the extra light out of the room.

He returned to the sofa and grabbed his laptop from the end table, opening the lid while sitting down again. The young girl lightly snoring a few feet away reminded him that he needed to come up with a plan. Following what he normally did when he was stressed, he loaded the webpage of Eliza's videos. After making sure the volume was low, he opened the recording of Eliza's recent live video. In the list of comments below the loading box, he found the one he added while waiting in the parking lot of E's Auto Body and Repair, before everything happened.

I could have used this information earlier. It would have saved me a busted hose. PS: Where's your Supra? PPS: You should definitely do another live video. PPPS: I can't wait to see you.

He settled deeper into the seat and closed his eyes while listening to Eliza walk through the installation of the voltage gauge.

"Ms. Banding, do not try to call this person yourself," Officer Chapel said to Eliza. "We'll handle it, okay? They're likely dangerous."

Eliza nodded.

"We'll let you know if we hear anything. Will you be okay on your own while I take this information back to the station?"

"Yes," Eliza responded. She looked up at the officer towering over her. "Thank you. I'll call a friend."

"Good night, Ms. Banding, and I'm sorry again." Officer Chapel turned on his heels and walked out of the shop.

Eliza reached for her phone and dialed the first number on the screen.

CHAPTER 37 - The Comments

"Hey, E. Look at this." Allie was behind the desk in the shop's lobby, clicking the mouse of the computer. Her chin rested on her other hand while her eyes squinted at the screen.

"Allie, I appreciate you coming and hanging out with me, but I'm not really interested in any funny videos right now."

After the last police car left, Eliza didn't want to go back to her place and confront her brother and sister-in-law. She sent Johnny a message, telling him she was going to stay at the shop in case Nilah returned on her own, and that he and Lindsay should remain at her apartment for the same reason. Needing someone to talk to, she called Allie, hoping she wasn't interrupting the rest of her assistant, and best friend's, evening. Before Eliza could even finish telling the entire story, she heard keys jingling on the other end of the line and a car door open and close. Faster than Allie should have been able to arrive back to the shop, the lobby door opened and she walked through. Eliza filled her in on the rest of the details, prompting Allie to go straight to the computer and start clicking around.

"Not just any funny video. Your video." Allie realized her word choice immediately and slowly peeked over the computer monitor toward Eliza to see if there would be any repercussions. "Just come."

Eliza picked herself up from the hard chair in the waiting area, groaning through the exhaustion overtaking her, and joined Allie behind the desk.

"Look at this comment under your live video." She pointed to a specific block of text on the screen.

"I can't. My eyes are too tired to focus."

"Near the end. It says 'Where's your Supra?'"

"What about it, Al?" Eliza was rubbing her eyes, squinting to read the words next to a blurry, silver icon.

"Who knows that you don't have your car?"

"You. Johnny." She paused to think. "Oli." Eliza immediately remembered telling Oliver that she traded vehicles with her brother while she had Nilah.

"Okay, but that's not Oli's profile picture."

"And how do you know that?" Eliza asked.

Allie cleared her throat. She realized this wasn't the time to make a joke about the cute guys that come and go through Eliza's shop and how she kept track of certain ones' interactions on Eliza's videos. And that separately, she sent direct messages to some of them on the side. "I know his profile picture. It's not this silver SUV. His is a red anime character."

"Silver SUV?" Eliza squinted as hard as her eyes would allow. "Can you make that picture bigger?"

Allie clicked the circle of the profile picture, causing the page to load a larger image. Once visible, it showed a more detailed shot of the rear side of a silver SUV: a Santa Fe.

"Fuck! That's him! That's who has Nilah!"

"I can't sleep," Lindsay said, curled up in a ball and hugging a throw pillow on the sofa in Eliza's apartment.

"I know, but at least rest. The police are looking for her." Johnny paced the living room of the apartment, going back and forth between the entry door and the sliding door to the balcony. "Eliza's at her shop, and we're here in case Nilah comes back."

"But what if she goes home?"

Johnny stopped and pondered the question. He shook his head. "She wouldn't know we were home yet, right? She would come here if anywhere at all."

Lindsay sat up from the sofa. "But she knows our house better. She would be able to find her way there." Nilah often told her parents that they made a wrong turn to go to their house when she didn't know that they were stopping elsewhere before heading home. "She's only been here once. I'm going to our place. I'll wait there."

Mouth open, but with no opposing argument, Johnny nodded and said, "Okay. I'll keep a look out here. Just keep your phone on."

"One time, John. One damn time I had it turned off when you needed to know what kind of bread to buy at the grocery store. Don't worry, I won't do *that* again." Her unusual annoyance toward her husband was a reaction to the fear for her daughter's safety. "I'll even keep it charged." She headed to the foyer.

Johnny stopped her mid-motion. Facing his wife while gripping her shoulders, he said, "She'll come home."

"I—" A tear rolled down her cheek. "Stop or I won't be able to see to drive home." She wiped off the moisture. "I know."

Johnny pulled her in tight and wrapped his arms completely around her small frame.

"I love you, Linds."

"I love you."

After receiving a kiss on her forehead, Lindsay went out the door, pausing to look around the front balcony and across the parking lot. The hope of seeing her little girl walking toward her quickly vanished.

CHAPTER 38 - His Opportunity

"Mister, I'm hungry."

A young girl was standing over him as his eyes cracked open. The shooting pain in his back from falling asleep on the hard springs of the motel room's couch didn't stop him from jumping back when he saw the sight.

Nilah stood in front of him, rubbing her eyes and stretching. She was unfazed by the reaction she caused.

Once the adrenaline rush subsided, and his eyes were open enough to understand the context surrounding him, he searched for his nighttime purchases. Finding them on the end table, he looked back and forth between the potato chips and trail mix, choosing the latter as a healthier breakfast choice. He began to pass the trail mix directly to the girl before abruptly stopping and pulling them toward his body. He opened the bag and then handed them over.

"I want waffles," the girl said.

"Sorry," he croaked. Clearing his throat to allow more words to come out uninterrupted, he added, "No waffles."

"But I want waffles."

He sat up, yawned to pop his ears, and squeezed his eyes tight. "I don't have any waffles."

"My daddy makes waffles. My aunt makes waffles. You can make waffles."

"I don't have any waffles." He looked around. "I don't have a kitchen." He used his hands to demonstrate the empty motel room.

"Then I want to go home."

At that, he was done with the conversation. He stood from the couch and walked into the small bathroom, shutting the door behind him. Going to the sink, he looked in the mirror, rubbed at the stubble coming in, then turned on the water. Splashing his face a few times, he took a deep breath.

A muffled voice came from the other side of the door. "I have to go to the bathroom."

He let out another deep breath while searching for the towel with his eyes closed. After drying his hands and face, he opened the door to find the young girl immediately on the other side, now staring up at him.

She pushed past him and headed straight for the toilet.

In a panic, he removed himself from the bathroom and quickly pulled the door shut. He thought about leaving the motel room, shutting the door behind him, and driving away, never to return again. He headed to the sofa, grabbing his keys and phone. While checking the time, he saw a screen full of missed calls and a slew of voicemails. He immediately deleted the voicemails from the numbers he didn't recognize, leaving one from the person who sold him the Integra. With the bathroom door still closed, he loaded the voicemail and listened.

"Hey—uh—"

There was a long pause. The guy on the other end of the line sounded nervous. Was the previous owner of the car going to try to buy it back? He gave it a good thought. He was anxious to leave this town now. Selling the car would wash his hands of the situation, at least once he figured out how to get rid of the girl.

"I was just wondering, uh—"

"Spit it out already," he yelled at the phone.

"Can I come see my, uh, your—"

The toilet flushing made him jump, causing his finger to slip over the button to stop the playback. He grumbled. Not wanting to listen to the blabbering on the recording again, he shoved the phone into his pocket.

The door to the bathroom opened before the young girl poked her head out, said, "Oops," and returned to the sink. She exited the bathroom with dripping fingers and stood on the threshold with her hands on her hips.

"Waffles or home," she said.

"No." He still didn't know what to do.

"Yes."

"No." He turned away from her and reached for the laptop on the couch. While closing the lid to put it on the end table, he didn't hear the tiny footsteps walk across the thinly carpeted Berber floor.

"Yes!"

He flinched when hearing the sound directly behind him. Spinning around, he crouched and yelled in the girl's face. "No!"

He wasn't entirely sure about the next couple of things that had happened. When his focus returned, his left shin was burning with pain and the nightstand was toppled over across the room. A large section of damaged drywall decorated the wall above the piece of furniture. His possessions were left scattered on the floor. The girl was unhurt, but wailing. He knew he had scared her.

Shit.

The rush of anger began to settle with the whining coming from the thing that had moved to the bed. He walked over near it, and slowly reached a hand out.

"Shhh. Okay. Uh. You're hungry, right?" He saw the bag of trail mix scattered across the floor. His hand clenched into a fist. A light breath later, and his fingers were outstretched again trying to calm the girl. "I'll go buy another candy bar. Do you want a candy bar?"

The girl's limbs began flailing wildly as his hand got closer to her. He stopped for fear of getting kicked again or scratched.

He racked his brain, trying to remember what else was in the vending machine. "I can buy another bag of trail mix. It's okay. That one was probably . . ." *Probably perfectly fine and now wasted.* "Probably stale. I'll get another."

The crying was getting louder, and he couldn't get his thoughts straight.

"Shut up!" he yelled out.

The momentary shock of his shouting silenced the girl for just long enough that he had false hope it had ended. Until the crying became screaming.

Realizing the thinness of the walls he shared with his motel neighbors, he went to the TV and plucked the remote from the top of it. The old bulb of the television struggled to life after he pressed the power button on the top of the sticky black device in his hand. He couldn't reach for the button to increase the volume fast enough. He continuously pressed it until the TV was at the same loudness as the girl. Conveniently set to a cartoon showing a princess petting a unicorn, the TV took the girl's focus to the moving picture. The screaming quickly ramped down to quiet sobs.

At the sight of the unicorn bumping its head on an apple tree and coming back with an apple sticking on its horn, the sobs turned to muted laughter and the girl sat up in the bed. She crossed her legs to get comfortable.

After a second bout of giggles, the girl finally made a noise that wasn't mixed with crying or screaming.

He couldn't hear her over the TV. He set the volume to a reasonable level and asked her, "What?"

"Cookies."

"Huh?" he said with an eyebrow raised.

"I want cookies."

He held up a finger before walking out the door and to the vending machine.

CHAPTER 39 - Closed

"Hey, Allie," Eliza whispered, trying to wake her assistant dozing across the chairs in the shop's lobby without scaring her. "Allie, hey."

"I don't wanna." Allie struggled to open an eye and looked at Eliza. "Just a few more minutes."

"There's no way you're not in pain from sleeping there." Eliza looked over her friend. A foot and hand were both hanging off the edge.

"I'm not thirty-five yet." Allie half stuck out her tongue. "I'll be okay."

"Yeah, yeah." Having celebrated the day after her own thirty-fifth birthday with an impressive hangover earlier in the year, Eliza responded by sticking out her own tongue. "Hey, look, I'm closing the shop to customers today. Go home. I'm staying here in case Nilah turns up."

"I'm not leaving you." Allie finally sat up, stretched her neck, and rubbed at her hip. "Keep the shop closed, but I'm staying."

"No, really, there's no point in you being here all—"

"Shut it." Allie stood, continuing to stretch. "Look, I'll go run out and get us something to eat. Definitely some coffee, but I'm coming back after that."

Knowing she lost the fight, Eliza kept her mouth closed. She sat in the seat next to the one Allie had just occupied and buried her face in her hands.

Allie reached out to Eliza. She patted her on the shoulder, comforting her friend in a minor but necessary way. "I'll be back in a few."

"Thanks," Eliza said into her hands. "Thank you."

Eliza's face remained buried for a few minutes after the shop's door swung shut; the bell used to alert her to people coming and going, having since stopped jingling. Her phone rang. Initially wanting to ignore it and remain in her misery, a light flickered in her mind that it could be the police calling to tell her that they had found Nilah, or even better, that Nilah had made it to Johnny and Lindsay.

"Yes?" Eliza said into the phone before her finger had even left the button she used to answer it.

"Eliza, hey, it's Eric."

Eliza pulled the phone away from her ear and looked at the screen. *Eric's Automotive* was displayed across the top of the device. She returned the phone to her ear. "Eric, hey, um, I can't—"

"When those kids, or whoever, took my toolbox, they must have grabbed my only hose remover tool. I hate to bug you, but you said if I needed something to call."

"Now's not a great time. I'm waiting on a—"

"It's this stubborn hose on this Integra. It's stuck. I should have removed it before the part came in, and now I'm late getting it back to its owner because the new hose came late. I had it over the weekend, and he should have had it back yesterday. If I had checked sooner, I would have known I was missing the tool so I—"

This time Eliza interrupted Eric. "A what?"

"Hose remover tool. You know, with the hook on the end?"

"No, not the tool. What car?"

"Oh. An Integra. I'm sure you've seen it around. The guy brought it to the shop a couple days ago."

Dumbfounded and at a loss for words, Eliza let Eric continue talking.

"He said he busted the hose while trying to install a gauge of some sort. Voltage maybe. I don't know. There's one in there. It looked like a pretty clean install. Either way, I need to get this done. So, got the tool I can borrow?"

"Eric," Eliza said slowly and deliberately, making sure she had his full attention. "What color is the Integra?" Part of her hoped she already knew the answer while the other part of her wished for a much different outcome. She remembered that the owner of the Sante Fe mentioned a busted hose in the comment they left on her live video.

"Silver. Scuff on the back. Why? Know the guy? It wouldn't surprise me. You get most of the business around here."

The phone slid out of Eliza's hand. It bounced off the seat of the chair and landed face down on the black and white checkered floor.

"Eliza?" she heard from the slight amplification of the hard surface. "Eliza? Are you there? That was a joke."

Trembling, Eliza picked up the phone, carefully held it between two hands, and pressed it against her ear. "I need—" Her voice shook. "I need to know where the guy is."

"Why?" Eric sounded confused. "Does he owe you money? Is that why he came to my shop and not yours? He'll pay, right? The part didn't cost much, and I'm sure I'll get another car in here that needs it someday, but I'd still hate to be out the money up front."

"My niece."

There was a moment of dead air before Eric finally responded with a single word. "Huh?"

Eliza's face returned to its earlier position in her palms. With one hand still clutching the phone, and her voice slightly muffled, she carefully enunciated her words. "*He has my niece.*"

"Why?"

"She disappeared last night from my shop. He was here. He drove away with her in his car."

"But I have his car." Eric sounded skeptical. "How could he possibly?"

"He has another. A Santa Fe. It was here last night." Suddenly, the words started spewing out of her like an open faucet relieving built-up pressure. "Nilah and I were playing hide and seek. Well, she was playing hide and seek. I didn't know. I couldn't find her. I ended up outside as a silver Santa Fe like his drove away. I haven't seen her since, and I don't know where she is. The police are looking for her. My brother is waiting for her to come home. I'm just sitting in my shop helpless." As the faucet began to run empty, she started sputtering. Slow coughs bubbled up, causing her to choke as the few tears she was able to release started to form in her eyes.

"Um. Eliza." Eric paused, waiting for an acknowledgement. "Eliza? Do you know this guy? Why would he have your niece?"

"I don't know!" As Eliza was thinking through an explanation, anger took hold, and her voice became stronger and louder. "This guy hurt me. He attacked me. And I don't know why. And now he has Nilah."

"Did you . . . uh . . ."

Eliza could tell Eric was holding back a question. "What? Did I *what?*"

"Did you damage one of his cars?" he blurted out.

"No! I don't know him. I know he watches my videos."

"Did he not like something you said in one of your videos?"

"Dammit, Eric. I don't know." She threw her head back, narrowly missing the sharp edge of the top of the plastic chair. "But you have his car, and now I can find him."

"I guess."

"What do you mean 'you guess'? Eric, I need your help."

"Okay. I don't— Sure. What do you want me to do?"

"Make him come back to your shop so I can bash his head open with a pry bar." Eliza's anger at her attacker, and now Nilah's kidnapper, had her threatening actions she would have never considered prior.

"But what if he doesn't have your niece? Or doesn't bring her with him? Or what if—" It was obvious to Eliza that Eric had stopped himself from saying something that would have upset her further.

"No. Don't even think about that last 'what if.' What do you suggest then? Do you know where he is? Oliver said the guy doesn't even live here."

"Who's Oliver?"

"The owner of Grinded Beans. How do you not know him? That Integra was his. He sold it to this guy. So, what better idea do you have?"

"Okay. Look. I don't know if this will work. The guy seemed fine every time I talked to him, but what if I take the car back to him?"

"Wait. Eric. Do you know where he is? Why the fuck didn't you tell me that? Give me the address. I'm going there now." Eliza popped out of her seat and was halfway to the door to leave her shop before Eric had a chance to respond.

"No, I don't. But what about this? Can you bring that tool over? I'll get the car fixed, call him up, and tell him I'll bring it to him. He told me he could walk back to wherever he is, so it's got to be close to here."

Eliza was listening, contemplating the suggestion.

"I can offer it up as an apology for being late getting the car back to him."

"Apologize my——" Eliza cleared her throat. "I don't hate this." She was now pacing around the lobby of the shop, deciding if she wanted to sit again, or dig out the tool Eric needed and start the drive over to his shop. "Does he still need to pay? You didn't charge him already? Right? I never——" Eliza stopped. It wasn't any of her concern about how another shop owner's business was run.

"I already tol——" Eric paused. "Yes, he still needs to pay. But I'll handle that. Okay?"

"Okay. Sure. Yeah."

"Okay. Now, can you bring by that tool?"

Stubborn was the only word Eliza could think of to respond with, but settled for, "I'll be over in a few."

CHAPTER 40 - Cookies for Breakfast

He watched the little girl happily eat the bag of cookies he gave her while he opened a second package for himself. Taking them out one-by-one, he popped each into his mouth.

The TV had silenced the girl's crying, and the junk food was keeping her mouth too occupied to talk. He took the opportunity to begin planning how to return the girl, or at least leave her somewhere where he could be rid of her. The first thought was to take the girl back to E's Auto Body and Repair, and leave her at the front door. He grabbed his phone to check the time and mumbled a quiet swear when he realized that the shop itself would already be open for business. Even if it wasn't, there might still be a police car waiting.

While willing the time to do something that would help him—either go backward, or speed up—the phone began vibrating. His eyes shot open wide when he momentarily thought he had elicited the movement from the device. The screen display changed, showing a phone number he recognized as the shop that was working on his secondary vehicle. He hovered his thumb over the button to end the call, then decided there was little harm in finding out what the mechanic needed. To alleviate the risk of ending the girl's silence sooner than he wanted, he sped toward the bathroom, and shut the door behind him while he answered the call.

"Hello?"

"Hi! Sir! Good news."

He wondered how the guy on the other end of the line sounded so awake. "Yes?"

"Ahem. Sorry. Hello. This is Eric. Eric's Automotive. I have your car. Your Integra."

"Okay?"

"Ah, yes. Good news. I have the part. It won't take me but an hour to get it replaced. For your patience, I'd like to bring the car to you when it's done. You mentioned you were close by. I could stand the walk back to the shop after dropping it off. No worries at all. None. Nope."

"Sure?" He didn't need the car anytime soon. And it was the least of his concerns, especially right now.

"No trouble at all. If you want, you can just pay over the phone."

"I don't really—"

"I, ahem, uh, for the trouble, I'll knock off a couple buck-a-roos."

Buck-a-roos? "I— Sure, man. Whatever." If the car was dropped off, he wouldn't have to leave the motel room. Not until he headed home, and certainly not before the young girl was gone. He patted his pockets. Finding them all empty, he said, "Hey, I need to find my wallet."

"Yup. Yes. Yeah. No rush. I'll wait."

He wondered if this guy drank far too much coffee in the mornings. Coffee. He needed some of that, too. After he tracked down his wallet, that was going to be his next goal. Stealing himself away from the bathroom, he found his target on the sofa. He was surprised to see the girl still sitting cross-legged on the bed with her eyes focused on the TV. One hand was holding the apparently-empty cookie bag, while the other rested inside of it. A flicker of light from the TV caught his eye and he turned to see that the girl was watching a classic cartoon from when he was a kid. He backed away slowly and returned to the bathroom.

Placing his phone to his ear, he said, "I got it. Ready?"

"Yessir. Ready Freddy."

After clarifying the total amount owed, yet still bitter that he needed to get the car fixed in the first place, he read the credit card numbers to Eric.

"Great, great, great," Eric said. "Now, just tell me where to drop off the car, and I'll get it over to you as soon as a lion gets, well, however that goes."

"I don't know the address."

"Um. Okay?"

"You know the motel off of, I think it's Devon Road. Or Street? It's near the lake." He was far from prepared to tell someone how to find him.

"Avenue? Horseshoe Motel?" Eric clarified.

"Probably."

"Yeah. Okay. I'll bring it there. Which room? I'll hand you the keys. Make sure, you know, you get them."

The question made him pause. He didn't want to open the door to the motel room while anyone was around. He racked his brain to find an excuse. "I, uh, hey, just leave the keys in the car in the lot. Yeah? It'll be fine there."

"I don't . . . I don't know, man. It can be sketchy in those motel lots. I really think I should hand you your keys. You know, in person."

Having had extra time to think, he decided he definitely didn't want to see anyone in person in the current situation he was in. "Eric?" For a moment, he wondered if he had the right name. The pause allowed the man on the other end of the line to confirm.

"Yes?"

"I don't know that I'll be here." He tried to sound firm, while hiding the annoyance in his voice. "Just do what I say. I'm all settled up, right? Just drop the car off in the lot when you're done. I'll deal with the consequences. Intended or not."

There was silence on the other end of the line.

"Right?" He sounded more forceful on his follow-up.

"Ye— Yes. Okay. Right. Thank you, sir."

"Right." In an attempt to put the mechanic's mind at ease, he added, "Just text me after you drop it off. I'll make sure to get it locked up as soon as I can."

"Sure. Yeah. Okay. Bye."

"Bye."

The phone line remained open on the other end of the call. He wondered if Eric had more to say and what response he may need to use. After another moment, he tapped the button on his phone to end the call.

CHAPTER 41 - Nilah's Born

6 Years Prior

"*Aunt* Eliza." Johnny made sure to emphasize the new title bestowed upon his sister. "I'd like to introduce you to Nilah Teagan Banding."

Eliza readjusted herself on the sofa in Johnny and Lindsay's six-month-old home and held out her arms, waiting for the new family member to be delivered to her.

Johnny gently placed his newborn daughter in the crooks of Eliza's arms and folded the hanging blanket back over Nilah's pink legs.

The nervousness of holding the tiny baby quickly subsided as the creeping smile on Eliza's face began to touch her ears. She ignored the sound of the camera shutter from Lindsay's phone as she stared down at her niece for the first time.

"Oh. Oh, oh, oh," Eliza suddenly let out in a hushed tone. "I have something for her." She nodded her head toward the large bag sitting on the floor in front of the sofa. "I hope it fits." She went back to adoring the girl in her arms.

Johnny picked up the bag and handed it to Lindsay. His wife was still sore from having only just returned home from the hospital after giving birth to their daughter. "This is heavy. What did you put in here?" he asked.

Lindsay pulled out the first piece of tissue paper, smiling at the tiny cars covering the thin material. "How appropriate," she said, directed at her sister-in-law. "How long did it take you to find this?"

"Not long, but keep going." Eliza's voice couldn't hide her excitement for the new parent to see what was inside.

Lindsay reached in and pulled out the first prize; a onesie with a pattern of a pair of mechanic's coveralls, oil splotch designs spread across the front.

"This is *sooo* cute," Lindsay said, holding it outstretched. She looked at the label inside. "It'll fit her in a few months. Thanks, Eliza." She continued turning the outfit around, poking at the small details: a blank name tag to write on and fake stitched pockets.

"You want her turning wrenches with you already?" Johnny asked his sister. "At least give her a couple years."

"Just wait till you see what else is in there," Eliza responded. Her eyes didn't move from Nilah's fuzzy red head. "John, help Lindsay out."

Johnny reached his hand inside the bag and pulled out a wooden car. Its pieces were held together with large plastic bolts. Attached to the sides were plastic screwdrivers and wrenches. "Yes, yes you do," he said. He held the toy out so Lindsay could get a better look.

"Yes. Yes, I do," Eliza repeated.

"Now, about that real car you showed up in," Johnny started. "I'm going to guess there's no room for car seats in there?"

Eliza laughed. "No, sorry, that was not my initial thought when I went over to the dealership. I fell in love with it at first sight." Eliza moved her head closer to Nilah's. "But not quite as much as I'm falling in love with this face. Guys, you made a beautiful baby girl. I love her already."

"But uh . . ." Johnny tried to return the conversation back to the vehicle. "Can I take it for a spin?"

"Sure. Keys are by my shoes near the front door." Eliza didn't care about anything else going on in the world while she was holding her niece.

Johnny immediately began walking toward the entrance to the house.

Lindsay looked up at her husband. "Do not crash your sister's new car, please. I need you to change the diapers tonight. And I don't think we can afford the repair bills while I'm at home for the next few months."

"I'll just make him freelance at my shop to fix it," Eliza said. "You know, when he's not at work, here with you and Nilah, or sleeping. It'll be fine."

"How you still manage to make a dig at me without even looking in my direction is an incredible skill," Johnny retorted.

"One of many I have, and you know it." Eliza broke her eye contact with her niece long enough to look at her brother and give him a wink.

"Yeah, yeah. Anyway, I'm taking your Supra out for a drive. Thanks, sis." He swung the front door open to go check out Eliza's new vehicle parked in the driveway. "I'll miss your Celica, but phew, that white is *bright*."

"I'd tell you that you better bring it back, but I know you'd rather spend time with this girl here." Eliza realized her mistake as soon as the sentence left her mouth. Knowing she wasn't clear about whom she meant, she waited for Johnny to get the last words in as he walked out the door.

"I spent two thirds of my life with you. It's time to spread my wealth. Bye!"

The door shut behind Johnny, shaking the house.

Lindsay eased up from her chair and moved to join Eliza and Nilah.

"Feeding time?" Eliza asked. She began moving her arms toward Lindsay to hand her Nilah.

"Not yet. You can keep her for a little bit longer."

Eliza's smile remained wide. "I can't wait to watch this little girl grow up."

"Me neither," Lindsay replied. She eased a finger into her daughter's tiny fist.

The squeal of a car's wheels outside the front of the house broke the cherished discussion between Eliza and her sister-in-law.

"I'm gonna yell at him when he gets back," they both said in unison.

After a quick giggle, Eliza added, "I guess he hasn't driven a clutch in a while?"

"Probably not since I last did. Right before we got engaged." Nilah squirmed, causing Lindsay to reach out her hands. "I guess it *is* feeding time."

After a quick kiss on baby Nilah's forehead, Eliza gently transferred her niece over to Lindsay's waiting arms. "See you soon, sweet girl."

CHAPTER 42 - The Competition

Eliza dropped the hose removal tool onto the passenger seat of her brother's CR-V and sent a message to Eric letting him know she was on her way.

In one motion, she shifted the car into drive while calling Johnny and putting the phone on speaker. She was happy when he picked up immediately, until he asked his first question.

"Do you have her?" His voice was excited, yet cautious.

"No. Sorry. I— No. But hey, I'm heading over to Eric's so he can take the car back to the guy that has Nilah." The wheels on the CR-V broke traction, letting out a small squeal as Eliza turned out of the shop's parking lot and onto the main street.

"What?"

"Shit, sorry." Eliza quickly explained her theory to Johnny and why she was heading to another automotive repair shop. "Meet me there," she told him.

"I don't have a car."

"What the hell, John. Why? Where is it?"

"Linds went home. She took the car. I stayed at your place. She wanted to wait at ours in case Nilah came home, you know?" The hope in his voice had completely fallen. "Who's going to be at your shop in case Ni goes there?"

"Right, yeah, okay. Allie's back at the shop. She said she'd wait there for me. But crap, um, I need to call the police. You call Lindsay, okay? Get over to Eric's Automotive. I'm going to see what Eric needs to get this done quickly. I don't even know if that car is drivable right now, but I think we're going to need all the help we can get."

"Yeah. Okay. Eric's Automotive. That's not far from your shop?"

"Right." She hung up before either could say goodbye. After making sure she was going to make it through the next intersection without a collision, she dialed the number that Officer Chapel called her from. The phone rang over and over with no indication that it would be picked up.

She continued into the lot of Eric's Automotive while listening to the repetitive sound from the speaker of her phone. Once parked, she ended the call, grabbed the tool from the seat next to her, and ran into the shop.

"Eric!" she yelled out. "Let's get this done."

"In the back," Eric responded. "You know your way."

Once in the garage bay, she found Eric with his head under the hood of what was once Oliver's Integra, trying to yank off the busted hose. When Eric looked up at her, she held out the tool, briefly in a way that she would have if she was trying to gut a victim; the hook end pointed straight at his chest.

"Do you know where this guy is?" Eliza asked in an almost threatening manner.

"Yeah. Horseshoe Motel. By the lake." He reached his hand out, moving his fingers to indicate he was ready for the tool.

Flipping it around so that she was now holding the hook end, Eliza plopped the handle into Eric's hand. "That's not far from here. God, I hope she's there. I hope she's—" She sniffled as tears threatened to escape.

"Hey. Stop. All right? I'm sure she's fine." Eric stuck his head further in the engine compartment. "This shouldn't take long now."

"Where's the new hose?" Eliza was looking around the car, trying to find what part was needed after the old hose was removed.

"Cardboard box." Eric grunted while popping the tool into place. "On the ground, other side of me."

Eliza found the box that was slightly obscured by Eric's legs. She went around, picked up the open container, and removed the short black hose. Examining it by flipping it around and spinning it, she asked, "How did this guy even manage to break the other one?" Her curiosity as a mechanic couldn't be held back.

"Don't know." Eric tossed the busted tube behind him, narrowly missing Eliza. After she yelped, he apologized. "Sorry, I'm not used to having anyone else in here." He held out his hand with the tool as a silent gesture for Eliza to take it. When she did, he kept his hand open, waiting for the new hose to fill his empty palm. She complied and began spinning the tool around in her hands, impatiently waiting for Eric to finish.

"Got it!" he yelled. "Keys are on the driver's side if you want to fire it up for me."

Eliza picked up the key ring and dropped down into the seat. The sudden realization of whose car she was sitting in made her shudder.

"I'm ready," Eric said. "In better circumstances, we'd make a great team."

After putting the key in the ignition, Eliza turned it and heard the car come to life.

"He said it was idling weird, so give it a minute," Eric called.

"I don't have a minute. Come on, man. Let's get going."

CHAPTER 43 - Horseshoe Motel

Lindsay pulled into the parking lot of Eliza's apartment complex and found Johnny waiting for her under the building's awning.

Once he noticed his wife's car, he quickly made his way to the passenger side and jumped in. "Eric's Automotive," he said, pulling the seatbelt across his body.

"Where's that?" Lindsay asked him, deadpan.

"Make a left out of the parking lot."

"Eliza knows where Nilah is?" Lindsay asked. Her eyes remained focused on the road in front of her.

"She thinks she does, yes."

"I hope she's right. I want my little girl back."

"Next left, and through the next light."

"I didn't sleep at all last night. Every sound that I heard I thought was her little footsteps coming to tell us that she needed a drink of water, or that her stuffie fell out of bed, or that—" Lindsay lost her train of thought as her eyes began to well up.

Johnny reached over and put his hand on his wife's leg. He squeezed it lightly. "We have to hope, Linds."

Lindsay nodded. A sniffle was the only noise she made.

"Turn right at the next intersection."

Lindsay followed the instructions. She wiped at her eyes after straightening out the steering wheel.

"See where that silver car is pulling out of? That's where we're going."

Eliza was sitting in the passenger seat of the Integra while Eric pulled the car out of the shop's parking lot and onto the main road. She closed her eyes briefly, imagining how the next scene was going to unfold.

Having rushed to leave Eric's shop, Eliza was still holding the hose remover tool in her hand. She was spinning it around like a tennis racket with her arm jerking slightly while daydreaming about making Nilah's kidnapper pay.

Eliza's buzzing phone brought her back. When she saw Johnny's name on the screen, she silently cursed herself.

"John, shit, I'm sorry," she said after answering it.

"Did I go to the right place? We're at Eric's. We've been looking around, but you're not here."

"Yeah, we must have left right before you got there. We're headed to that old motel near the lake. I think it's the one with the playground that you took Nilah to."

Eliza heard Johnny relaying the information to Lindsay. Directed back at Eliza, he said, "Okay, we'll go there."

Eric tapped Eliza on the shoulder.

Speaking to her brother, Eliza said, "John, I'll see you over there."

Eliza turned to see what Eric wanted after disconnecting the call. She followed his pointing finger to the lake a block ahead of them. The sign for the motel was half lit and she could see the other half flickering even in the daylight.

"Almost there," Eric said, unnecessarily. "What's your plan?"

"Shit."

"I don't think taking a sh—" Eric stopped himself from making a joke at her word choice. "How about you hop out of the car before we get to the parking lot. I'll pull off and let you out. Just in case he's around, I don't . . . we don't want him to see a second person in his car."

"He also knows my face if he's been watching my videos."

"That too." Eric slowed the car, looking for a good drop-off spot for Eliza. "I'll go park his car in the parking lot and look like I'm walking away. We can keep an eye out for which motel room he leaves when he comes to get the keys from the car."

Eliza looked at Eric in awe. His plan didn't seem half bad and he was staying with her through the entire process. Scanning the parking lot of the motel as they pulled closer, she noticed a silver Santa Fe parked halfway in, on the side with the motel room doors. "Hey." She pointed a finger across Eric's line of sight. "That's his other car. The Santa Fe over there."

"Then he's probably in one of the rooms near it." Eric went silent, an indication that he had an idea.

"What, Eric? What are you thinking?"

"I think I'll park away from his other car. I'll put it close enough that he'd be able to see it out of one of the windows, but far enough that he'll be out of the motel room for a few extra seconds." Eric slowed the Integra to a stop against a curb just outside the entrance of the motel's parking lot.

Eliza said a silent prayer to herself. She carefully opened the car door, checking traffic before stepping into the street to walk around the vehicle and to the sidewalk. She patted the hood of the car, indicating to Eric that she was out of the way and he could proceed with the plan.

While watching Eric ease the car into the parking lot, Eliza walked into the lot, hugging the line of motel rooms and keeping her back turned to the windows.

Eric appeared to be making a show of returning the Integra. He drove it past the Santa Fe, made a three-point turn at the end of the dead-end lot, and turned back. He passed the Santa Fe a second time and positioned the car to back into an open space. He kept the front of the vehicle facing the motel room doors.

Eliza grinned slightly at the customer service Eric was providing when he picked a spot that had no other surrounding vehicles, leaving empty parking spots on both the driver and passenger sides of the Integra. Once the car was stopped, she impatiently waited for Eric to get out of the car. "Come on, come on, come on," she said aloud, nearly bouncing for him to get moving.

Watching Eric crawl out of the short vehicle, his six-foot-tall frame appearing to tower over it once he stood completely upright, she waited to see which direction he would go. He gently closed the door, causing Eliza to bow her head in slight frustration at his slowness. Eric finally walked toward the entrance of the parking lot. She stopped, not sure what to do, realizing that if he walked directly over to meet her near the motel room doors, it could appear suspicious.

She saw Eric stop and remove his phone from his pocket. The few quick thumb presses on the screen indicated to her that he was typing something. Wondering if he was sending her a message, Eliza stuck her hand in her pocket and wrapped her fingers around her phone, waiting for it to buzz. Nothing came. She realized the communication must have been intended for the vehicle's owner.

Eric continued to the entrance of the parking lot before crossing over to Eliza's side. He doubled back to meet her.

CHAPTER 44 - His Escape

He heard his phone chirp in his pocket. Setting the laptop aside where he had been watching another of Eliza's videos to keep himself calm, he fished the device from his pocket, knowing that the mechanic was due to return his Integra.

Just dropped off your car. Thanks for being an understanding customer!

Somehow the little girl was still quietly watching the TV. He was sure he had plenty of time to retrieve the keys from the car, lock it, and return before she even noticed. He peered out the front window of the motel to make sure Eric was gone and not sticking around to have a conversation that he didn't feel like having. He scanned the assortment of parked vehicles for a moment before he finally found the Integra.

"He had to put it way down there, didn't he?" He scoffed, annoyed, then went out the front door. Checking the parking lot for moving cars before he crossed to the other side, he started his walk to his new car.

A man and a woman were standing near the end of the motel, closest to the main road. They were far enough away that he couldn't make out any discernible features, but he still turned his head away to avoid making any eye contact with his temporary neighbors.

As he approached the Integra, a brand-new convertible pulled into the motel parking lot. The temporary tags on the glittering vehicle were still bright white. His eyes focused on the shine of the paint in the sun while he reached into his own new car and grabbed the keys from the center console. The convertible wasn't a car that belonged in the parking lot of a dingy motel. He didn't think he belonged in a dingy motel parking lot either, but that's where he currently found himself.

Just over the top of the car he saw another vehicle had followed it in. The red and blue lights sitting on the roof of the second car made it obvious what type of vehicle it was. It was likely that the police car pulled over the convertible. That seemed like a valid reason for it to be in this lot. Wanting no parts of what was about to come next, he locked his Integra and started his walk back to his motel room.

While moving toward the building, he noticed the couple from the end of the lot had begun running in his direction. He panicked, thinking they knew something more was afoot related to the two recently added vehicles in the lot. He broke into a run, too.

Keeping a distance just ahead of the two people, he glanced back toward the police vehicle. In that moment he was able to make out the faces of the man and woman. *Why is the mechanic still here? Why is he running in this direction?* He glanced at the woman.

"Shit!" he yelled out when he recognized Eliza. Even in plain street clothes, he knew her face anywhere. Why was she here? She wasn't supposed to be here. *He* was supposed to be at her place.

He picked up his speed and burst through the front door of his motel room. Slamming it shut behind him, he ran to the back of the room. He remembered the window. Tearing the blinds off the wall, he removed the security bar, unlocked the window, and threw it open.

"That was loud. I couldn't hear the TV," a voice from the front of the room said.

He looked toward the young girl. After taking a moment to think, he rushed to her, hooked an arm under her stomach, and snatched her off the bed.

She kicked and screamed, struggling to get out from his grip while he made his way to the window. He looked out and realized that he would be able to easily slip through it. Putting one leg over the ledge, and then his other, he made it outside and headed toward the lake with the young girl in tow.

Eliza shoved the door open, finding the room lifeless except for some papers blowing around from the breeze through the back window. A pile of new clothes sat on the floor next to a tipped over shoebox, black combat boots spilling out. The rest of the room was a mess.

Cautiously, Eliza looked around while Eric came in close behind her. The papers moved across an open laptop on the couch. She focused on the screen. Her own face stared back at her. "Nilah!" she screamed.

The room was too small for her to miss her niece. The only closed door hid a small closet. Eric eased toward it and opened it carefully. Finding nothing but a few empty hangers, he shook his head when Eliza looked at him.

After making it across the room, Eliza peered out the open window. A short distance away, she could see a man with a young girl held by his side. He was struggling to keep her still. The movement slowed him down as he approached the lake.

Eliza climbed out the window and broke into a run.

CHAPTER 45 - Hide and Seek Champion

"Lindsay, wait for the police," Johnny said to his wife as she was inching her way closer to the door that Eliza ran through.

"But I want my little girl!"

"Mr. Banding," a burly officer said to Johnny from the open car door of the police cruiser.

"Yes?" Johnny thought back to the call he received immediately after Eliza told him they needed to go to the motel. The officer on the line explained that Eliza had shared Johnny's phone number with him as the missing girl's father. After missing a call from Eliza and being unable to get a hold of her, he called Johnny in hopes of finding her. Johnny was able to tell the officer that Eliza was headed to the motel. The police officer, whose name Johnny could only remember was related to a church building, said he would meet them in the motel parking lot.

"Where did your sister go, Mr. Banding?"

"This way!" Lindsay screamed. She pushed through the half-open motel room door, causing Johnny and the officer to follow her in.

Lindsay entered the room as a man was climbing out the rear window. She turned back to the door and ran face first into her husband's chest.

"They went out the back," Lindsay said to the pair. She sidestepped them and ran off to go around the building.

"Lindsay!" Johnny called out after his wife. "Wait up! You don't know who's there."

Johnny and Officer Chapel chased Lindsay in hopes of stopping her from running into the unknown.

He found himself easing toward the inner edge of a horseshoe-shaped lake. His recollection of the body of water was muddied. He thought there were two smaller, separate lakes behind the motel. The illusion had been caused by a steep drop-off into the water at the middle portion of the lake. No longer having a way to continue forward, he stopped and glanced at a small sign on a nearby post.

Danger: Deep Water

No Swimming

The mechanic who fixed his Integra, and the woman whose videos he had been watching for the better part of a decade, had slowed their progression but were closing in on him.

"Eliza. I— I just want to talk," he whispered. She moved close enough to him to finally hear when he continued. "We can be together. We can be friends. We can be more."

"I don't know you," she yelled back. "I don't even know your name. Who are you? Why do you have my niece?"

"That wasn't my intention. I like your videos. I watch them all the time. I think I can help with them. I think I can help you." He reached out one hand, trying to grab onto a feeling that wasn't reciprocated.

Eliza stopped when he motioned to her. Eric followed her lead, putting himself one step ahead of her.

"Tell me—" He was looking for a way to get her to talk to him. "Tell me about your favorite video. Was it your first one? That was my favorite." He blushed admitting it. His grip on Nilah loosened involuntarily as his body relaxed at the thought of watching Eliza on his screen. The girl tried to pull away, reaching out to her aunt, until her feet left the ground.

Eliza's normal embarrassment at someone discussing her videos was overshadowed by her wanting to keep Nilah safe. She moved again, stepping closer. Looking down at the man's feet, she could make out the white tips of his shoes through the thick grass. The black stood out against the green.

"You! It *was* you in the elevator!" Eliza's pace suddenly quickened toward him. Her body language changed. Eric remained close, ready to help as needed.

The movement startled him. His tone changed in a moment. The soft discussion he tried to have with Eliza turned confrontational. "Stay back!" he yelled. Eliza suddenly became a threat to him. Not a friend. A foe. Not an image of beauty, but now a horror movie villain where he was the victim. Holding even tighter onto the young girl, he eased toward the edge of the lake. "I don't want to, but . . . But get away or . . ." A growl bubbled up from the back of his throat. "Or I'll . . ." He swung the girl around toward the water.

Nilah whimpered while being flung around like a rag doll.

His two new enemies were within reaching distance.

"Look. I mean it." He stepped again toward the water, inching closer and closer. "Please, don't. Don't!" he screamed.

"Let her go," Eliza demanded. "Why are you doing this?"

"I didn't mean to," he responded. "It wasn't on purpose. I rescued her. I was going to bring her back." His voice dropped to a whisper. "I'm a hero."

He closed his eyes. "I want you. I've always wanted you. I love you. Everything that you are. Everything that you share with me. It's your eyes." He opened his own to look at hers. "They want to tell me something. Something that they're holding back. They want to tell it to me. Just me."

"Bullshit. You hurt me." She pulled her hair aside, holding it in place. A finger pointed at the spot above her eye. "*You* did this." Eliza focused on Nilah. "And now you have her. I'm not going to say it again. Let her go."

He flinched at her use of profanity. Not once had he heard her curse around him or at him. He used it plenty, but her—never. She had a higher level of refinement. "That was . . ." He looked at the water, then to the little girl teetering on the high ledge. The gentle sound of the lapping water below stole his focus. "It was a mis—"

Eliza decided that she had given the man enough time to free Nilah. She made a dash and reached out for her niece.

He spooked. The incoming threat forced his decision. He shoved the girl off of the ledge and into the water. The splash from behind didn't take his attention away from Eliza. He prepared himself for a collision.

Yelling out with uncontrolled madness, Eliza adjusted her direction to aim for the man. She lowered her shoulder and dove. Eliza connected under his collarbone, throwing him off his balance. The momentum took them both over the ledge.

Eliza's arms wrapped around him as their weight carried them into the murky lake below.

"Nilah!" Lindsay cried out after seeing the large splash. She found herself next to Eric; both looking over the edge while trying to figure out how to help.

Nilah's head popped up out of the water. The young girl was treading in place, unable to touch the bottom of the lake. "Mommy!" she yelled when her eyes connected with her mother's.

Lindsay's maternal instincts took over. She jumped into the water and swam the short distance to her daughter. Grabbing onto a hand to help keep Nilah afloat, she asked, "Where's Aunt Eliza?"

"I don't know, Mommy. She fell in with the mean man."

Lindsay swam Nilah over to the edge of the lake as Johnny made his way to them. He reached over the ledge and grabbed onto one of Nilah's arms. With Eric's help, they were able to slowly pull her up onto the grassy area several feet above the water's surface.

"Linds, where's Eliza?" Johnny asked.

Lindsay could only shake her head in response. She wasn't able to make eye contact with her husband.

Struggling below the water, Eliza felt him pull at her in his attempts to bring himself to the surface. Every downward jerk caused her to grip onto the man and try to do the same in return. Each success of breaking free was immediately negated by the other's motions.

Eliza hoped that she had taken a deeper breath than he did as they went off the edge. Feeling her own lungs beginning to ache, she recognized that the man's struggle was finally slowing. She made another attempt to burst upward until her head snapped back. Her hair felt like it was being pulled from her scalp. The sensation caused Eliza to yell out in pain. Water rushed into her open mouth, stopping the sound from escaping. She gagged, barely able to see the bubbles escape from her in the murky water. She reached back and found the ends of her locks twisted around the man's clenched, motionless, hands. Eliza tightly gripped her hair and pulled. She felt more pain radiate through the back of her head. Unable to break free, the weight kept her down in the depths of the lake.

Lindsay held up her hand with only her index finger sticking up.

"Lindsay, what are you doing?" Johnny asked. Holding his daughter close, he kept his arms crossed over her wet body.

"Ma'am, please wait for the paramedics," Office Chapel called out over the lake's edge. "It's too risky. Let them do their job. It's been too long."

Lindsay stuck up a second finger.

"Lindsay, no, don't!" Johnny yelled, realizing she was about to ignore the officer's request.

A third finger went up. Lindsay's body tucked in on itself as she shot under the water's surface.

"Mommy!"

EPILOGUE

"Nilah, dear. Please stop crying. I know you're sad," Lindsay said to her daughter.

Nilah stood in her black dress. The petals of the small red satin rose attached to the belt around her waist were vibrant against the dark fabric. Through sobs, Nilah said, "Why. Can't. Aunt. Eliza. Be. Here."

Lindsay wrapped her arms around Nilah in an attempt to both comfort her and move her out of the way of the others walking past. All were wearing similar dark-colored outfits.

"I. Don't. Under. Stand," Nilah continued.

"I wish she was here, too. She would have loved to see you all dressed up, but she just can't be here." Lindsay tried to word her explanation clearly so that Nilah would understand. "Aunt Eliza and Mr. Eric flew to Texas for a car show. Everything was booked before your Halloween concert was scheduled," Lindsay said to reassure her. "I promised her that I would record the whole thing, and when she's back, you two can have a sleepover and watch it together. Okay?"

Nilah nodded as the sobs subsided.

"Now, can you wipe away the tears and go stand next to Daddy for a picture?"

Johnny reached out an arm as he stood at the entrance to Nilah's school, waiting for his daughter to join him. After she approached, he took the time to straighten her bow, then stood and faced Lindsay. She pointed the camera toward them. Once he heard the shutter click, he ushered his wife over so they could trade places for her to stand in the limelight with Nilah.

"Thanks for taking the trip out here with me, Eric." Eliza peeked in the window of the new model year Supra. "Before we head out, I need to see if any of the merchandise vendors have child-sized coveralls."

"Sure thing, and of course. I love cars as much as you."

"As much as *I* do?" she asked. "No one loves them as much as I do."

"Not quite what I meant, but sure, let's go with that." Eric stood beside Eliza and wrapped his arm around her waist.

"Excuse me," a young woman's voice behind them said.

They turned around, expecting to find someone waiting to get a closer look at the car they had been hogging.

"Are you, um—" The shyness was evident. "Are you Eliza? At E's Auto Body and Repair? Like the videos?"

"I am?" Eliza answered in question. She moved herself closer to Eric.

"I've been watching your videos since I was a teenager," the woman began. "They made me want to grow up and be like you. I started changing my own oil and rotating my tires and now I'm in charge of all of the cars in this section." The woman waved her hands around the area that the three of them were standing in and then pointed to the car logo on her polo shirt.

Eliza allowed her body to relax. After trading looks with Eric, she responded, "That's really amazing." Placing a hand across her chest in sincerity, she added, "Thank you for telling me that. I really needed to hear it."

"I haven't seen any new videos lately. Are you working on a big project?" the woman asked excitedly.

"I, well, needed to take a break, but I'm sure something new will come along eventually."

"Okay! Well, I can't wait. Anyway, I just wanted to say hi and thank you." She took notice of the car that Eliza and Eric were standing next to. "I think the Supra that you did the PPF wrap on was my favorite. It showed how much you treat each car like it's your own."

Eliza grinned. It was her favorite video too, but she kept the reason—it being her own car—held back. "It was really nice to meet you," she said.

The woman waved and then walked away.

Eliza turned and looked Eric in the eyes. "That was adorable, but I'm surprised she recognized me."

With his free hand, Eric brushed Eliza's newly-short hair away from her face. "I guess, but I do like your hair like this."

"Well—" Eliza thought back to the pain she endured when sections of her hair were broken and ripped out. The extra help needed from Lindsay to break free of the grasp of her stalker left parts of her hair mismatched. She didn't want to explain it on her next video, whenever that may be, and decided a new haircut was in order. "Thank you," she replied.

"Let me know when you're done ogling over this car and we'll go see what others are around." Eric gently patted the limited-edition anniversary Supra on the roof.

"As long as I don't see a classic Integra sitting here, I'll be fine with whatever."

ABOUT THE AUTHOR

Brian has an overabundance of hobbies—including some that crop up in his writing—and ventured into publicly releasing his stories several years ago. After being fascinated by the process, he continued with no end in sight.

He was an automotive enthusiast in a previous life and the work Eliza completes in *Consequences Intended* is just a small sampling of his knowledge. He misses his small two-door convertible Toyota.

Visit the link in the QR code below for more of Brian's works, or connect with him on Instagram @brianjlynch_author.